Wizards

The Myths, Legends, & Lore

AUBREY SHERMAN

AVON, MASSACHUSETTS

Published by
Adams Media, a division of F+W Media, Inc.
57 Littlefield Street, Avon, MA 02322. U.S.A.
www.adamsmedia.com

ISBN 10: 1-4405-8288-2
ISBN 13: 978-1-4405-8288-2
eISBN 10: 1-4405-8289-0
eISBN 13: 978-1-4405-8289-9

Printed in the United States of America.

10   9   8   7   6   5   4   3   2   1

Library of Congress Cataloging-in-Publication Data

Sherman, Aubrey.
  Wizards / Aubrey Sherman.
      pages cm
  Includes index.
  ISBN-13: 978-1-4405-8288-2 (pob)
  ISBN-10: 1-4405-8288-2 (pob)
  ISBN-13: 978-1-4405-8289-9 (ebook)
  ISBN-10: 1-4405-8289-0 (ebook)
1. Wizards. I. Title.
  BF1589.S54 2014
  133.4'3--dc23
                                    2014021583

Interior images © Clipart.com, Wikimedia Commons (public domain),
iStockphoto.com, Dover Publications, and 123RF.
Cover design by Erin Dawson.
Cover images © Dover Publications.

This book is available at quantity discounts for bulk purchases.
For information, please call 1-800-289-0963.

ACKNOWLEDGMENTS

The author would like to thank Meredith O'Hayre, Bryan Davidson, and Skye Alexander for their considerable help and erudition. Without them, this project would not have been possible.

Contents

INTRODUCTION 6

PART ONE: The World of Magic 9

CHAPTER 1: Who Are Wizards? 10
CHAPTER 2: The Power of Magic 24
CHAPTER 3: A Wizard's Equipment 50

PART TWO: Great Wizards of History 65

CHAPTER 4: Merlin: The Once and Future Wizard 66
CHAPTER 5: Wizards of the West 82
CHAPTER 6: Wizards of the East 107

PART THREE: Wizards of Story 117

CHAPTER 7: The Wizards of Harry Potter 118
CHAPTER 8: Wizards on the Bookshelf 148
CHAPTER 9: Wizards on the Big and Small Screens 172
CHAPTER 10: Wizards in Games and Comics 191

CONCLUSION: Wizards All Around Us 216
INDEX 220

Introduction

At the center of our most fantastic, mystical, mysterious stories stands the figure of the wizard. On the border between light and shadow, he puts forth his strange powers and shapes and crafts the reality around him. From the beginning of humanity, when our ancestors crowded around fires and told one another stories, to today's world of computer-driven special effects, we've been fascinated by wizards.

In this book we'll explore the world of wizards and magic. It's a world filled with wonder, with good and evil, with great heroes such as Merlin, Nicholas Flamel, and Harry Dresden, and with horrifying villains such as Saruman, Circe, and Baba Yaga. We'll see how wizards have been portrayed in print, on the screen (both big and small), and in games.

Wizards are firmly ensconced in our lives. When the grandfather of roleplaying games, Dungeons & Dragons, hit store shelves in 1974, players could take on the role of a spellcasting wizard. Decades later, they're still doing it, not only in the latest edition of D&D but in video games as well. The fact is, we'd *like* to be wizards. Who wouldn't want to say a few words, toss some magic powder or herbs in the air, give a dramatic gesture, and conjure up something? Who wouldn't want to be able to magically transport herself to any place on the planet? Who wouldn't want to be a repository of strange and arcane knowledge— and carry a magic staff?

The sense of excitement that wizards can create has been reflected in popular culture. Tens of millions flocked to bookstores to read J.K.

Rowling's tale of a young boy named Harry Potter who discovers, to his lasting amazement, that he's a wizard, destined for the Hogwarts School of Witchcraft and Wizardry. Millions more poured into theaters to watch Gandalf the Grey challenge Sauron and the power of the One Ring in Peter Jackson's epic film series, The Lord of the Rings.

Now, let's join the inhabitants of these wondrous, far-off places and step into the world of wizardry. Let the magic begin!

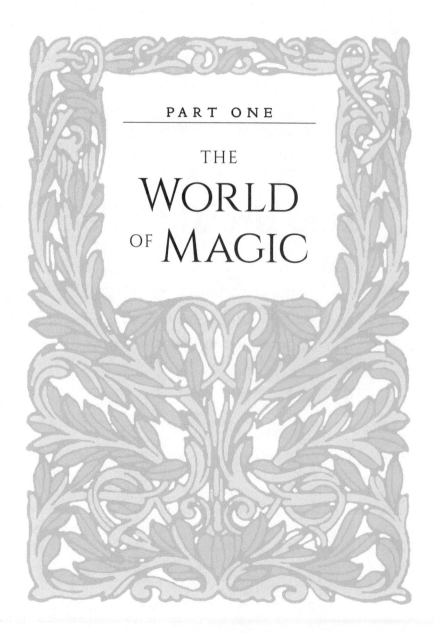

PART ONE

THE

WORLD
OF MAGIC

CHAPTER 1

Who Are Wizards?

"Do not meddle in the affairs of Wizards,
for they are subtle and quick to anger."

—GILDOR INGLORION, *THE LORD OF THE RINGS*
BY J.R.R. TOLKIEN

magine seeing a picture of someone wearing long, flowing robes and a tall, pointed hat covered in mysterious symbols. He carries a tall staff and possibly a shorter wand. He has a long, white beard and appears old but vigorous.

Most of us would have little difficulty in identifying this mysterious figure as a wizard. The aspiring wizards of Harry Potter's Hogwarts are required to purchase a set of wizard robes and a wand (there is no mention of pointed hats—perhaps these come later). Albus Dumbledore, the head of Hogwarts, certainly fits the picture described here.

But not all wizards look like this. They can be short, tall, thin, fat, old, or young. Some are men and others are women. They can dress in robes or wear jeans and T-shirts.

What's important about a wizard is not what she or he *looks* like but what the wizard *does*. Fundamentally, a wizard is someone who manipulates reality using magic. That's what links all these people together.

Of course, there are many different types and levels of wizards. These include:

◆ Adept	◆ Mystic	◆ Shaman
◆ Apprentice	◆ Necromancer	◆ Sorcerer
◆ Hedge wizard	◆ Seer	◆ Thaumaturgist
◆ Magus		

Some argue that alchemists are a type of wizard as well. Alchemy, which was widely studied in the Middle Ages and Renaissance, is the search for a way to turn base metals into gold. Although it shed much important light on what became the science of chemistry, it never succeeded in its object. On the other hand, many believe that this search is metaphorical and that what alchemists really seek is a wisdom beyond rationality.

THE LIFE OF A WIZARD

What sorts of things do wizards do?

A great deal depends on the context. In primitive societies, wizards were thought to be people who could channel magical forces through themselves, often going into trances to do so. In Lascaux, France, a series of caves were discovered in 1940. On the walls of the caves are paintings of animals; the paintings have been dated to the Paleolithic period, about 17,300 years ago.

Anthropologists have suggested that the paintings were created by tribal shamans as a means of enhancing the hunt—the animals depicted on the walls are typically the kind of creatures that would have formed a significant part of the Paleolithic diet. Many of the paintings are in the deepest and most remote parts of the caves where the most potent magic resided. (Similar cave paintings have been found at Altamira in Spain.)

These early tribal wizards played a central role in the well-being of their people. If their magic was sufficiently powerful, the hunt would be successful and the tribe was assured of a source of food. Some scholars have posited that the wizards went into trances prior to creating the paintings and in these trances they communicated with spirits from the Otherworld who blessed the success of the tribe's quest for food.

In more advanced societies as well as in stories, wizards had no need to play this role of ensuring the food supply would be uninterrupted. But many of their other functions are of equal importance.

- ◆ Wizards are the source of arcane wisdom, often written in spellbooks or handed down over the generations by word of mouth. Because of this, they often serve as counselors to rulers. Merlin played this role for King Arthur; John Dee was a court advisor to Queen Elizabeth I; and in David Eddings's novels,

Belgarath the Sorcerer advised numerous kings and princes on affairs of state.

* Wizards are powerful heroes, especially when matched against foes that would defeat lesser beings. In *The Fellowship of the Ring*, Gandalf alone can face the balrog on the Bridge of Khazad-dûm. "This foe is beyond any of you," he tells the other members of the Fellowship.

* Wizards can prophesy. In T.H. White's *The Sword in the Stone*, Merlin is able to see the future because he lives backwards in time (thus his past is our future). In Mary Stewart's novel *The Crystal Cave*, he can see in the flame of a candle things to come by communing with the Elder Gods. Not all wizards can do this, and some can only do it partially. Gandalf the Grey, for example, can see what's happening in various parts of Middle-earth and can foretell, in suitably vague terms, what's going to happen up to a point.

* Wizards can conjure things out of thin air. In C.S. Lewis's *The Voyage of the Dawn Treader*, the magician Coriakin, with a wave of his hand, causes a hearty dinner to appear for the crew of the *Dawn Treader*. Albus Dumbledore does the same thing for the hungry students of Hogwarts at their beginning-of-term feast in the Great Hall.

Because all of these are useful skills, wizards can often be found leading quests. Gandalf heads the Fellowship of nine companions in *The Lord of the Rings*; in David Eddings's Belgariad and Malloreon series of novels, the sorcerer Belgarath leads a company from place to place, searching for a stolen artifact. In Barbara Hambly's Darwath Trilogy, a wizard crosses time and space to our modern dimension to draw a student of medieval history into his world to help him.

THE DARK SIDE OF WIZARDRY

Because of their powers, wizards can also have dark sides. Gandalf warns Frodo Baggins in *The Fellowship of the Ring* of the danger that would ensue should he, Gandalf, take the Ring. He would, he says, "become like the Dark Lord himself," and it would start with his desire to do good. He knows, though, that the Ring would twist such a desire and ultimately render it into evil (later in the story we see an example of this when Boromir, wishing to gain the power of the Ring to save his beleaguered city of Minas Tirith, tries to seize the Ring from Frodo).

"The rollout of new technology always affects how wizards do business."

—DIANE DUANE

Some wizards and sorcerers are bad from the beginning—or at least only ambiguously good. Raistlin Majere, for example, the golden-skinned sorcerer of Margaret Weis and Tracy Hickman's Dragonlance series, abandoned his companions during their quest and ultimately donned the black robes of evil during the War of the Lance. Profion, the antagonist in the movie *Dungeons & Dragons,* is over-the-top evil, complete with cackling laugh and maniac expressions.

The Seduction of Evil

Just because Raistlin is evil doesn't mean the character hasn't been popular with readers. On the contrary, the character so intrigued fans that Weis and Hickman wrote a second trilogy of novels detailing Raistlin's conflicted relationship with his twin brother, Caramon Majere.

The attraction to evil for wizards comes from possessing power, which can make them arrogant, and from constantly living between the light and the shadow. One must keep in mind that from the wizard's standpoint, she or he is *not* evil. Morgan le Fay, a sorceress and Merlin's great opponent (depicted by Helen Mirren in the 1981 film *Excalibur*) is bitter with the wizard for manipulating her mother into sleeping with Uther Pendragon, thus conceiving Arthur. In revenge, she sleeps with Arthur, her half-brother, and by him conceives Mordred, who will eventually kill the king.

Even Voldemort, the evil wizard who killed Harry Potter's parents and is a brooding presence throughout the seven novels, believes that right is on his side. Wizards are superior to Muggles, he reasons, and so pureblood wizards should rule them. The fact that Voldemort himself is of mixed blood never seems to occur to him. All he knows is that he's got more talent than any other wizard. Of *course* he should be in charge.

Circe

On occasion, wizards go into exile, either voluntary or involuntary. Circe, a Greek enchantress who appears in Homer's *Odyssey*, was sent to the island of Aeaea, possibly for the murder of her husband. Once there, she received visiting sailors and turned them into animals to serve her. Among those who came to the island were Odysseus and his crew, returning from the Trojan War. She changed the Greek seamen into swine, but Odysseus, with some assistance from the gods, was able to force her to change them back again. Curiously, he then remained on the island for a year as her lover, drinking and generally enjoying himself.

The poet Hesiod, in a lost poem titled *The Telegony*, says that Circe had three children by Odysseus (presumably in Hesiod's version Odysseus remained on the island for longer than a year). To one of these, Telegonus, she gave a poisoned spear when he reached adulthood, and

with this spear the young man killed his father. He returned with Odysseus's widow Penelope and the hero's son by her, Telemachus. Circe, in atonement for the death of Odysseus, made them immortal.

Lycophron, who wrote in Greece during the third century B.C., recounts that Circe, grieving for Odysseus, brought him back to life with her magic. She then gave her daughter, Cassiphone, to Telemachus to be his wife. However, after some time Telemachus killed Circe and was, in turn, killed by Cassiphone. Upon hearing of this, Odysseus died of grief.

Circe Offering the Cup to Odysseus by John William Waterhouse (1849–1917)

"I have be-dimm'd
The noontide sun, call'd
forth the mutinous winds,
And 'twixt the green sea
and the azur'd vault
Set roaring war."

—PROSPERO, *THE TEMPEST* BY
WILLIAM SHAKESPEARE

Prospero

Shakespeare allows magic in only two of his plays: *A Midsummer Night's Dream* with its legion of fairies, and *The Tempest*. In this latter play, Prospero, the duke of Milan, is sent into exile by his usurping brother. On an island, Prospero studies magic in order to protect his daughter, Miranda. He uses his wizardry to enslave a creature, Caliban, while also drawing the loyalty of a spirit, Ariel, whom he has freed from imprisonment in a tree.

Prospero eventually draws his brother to the island, along with the king of Naples. He conjures a storm that wrecks their ship, stranding them on his island. However, his plans go astray when Miranda falls in love with Ferdinand, son of the king.

In the end, all is happily resolved and Prospero declares his intention to renounce his magic, as Miranda no longer needs his protection.

Prospero's magic, Shakespeare stresses, was undertaken for the sole purpose of protecting his daughter. Thus at the end of the play he declares:

"I'll break my staff,
Bury it certain fathoms in the earth,
And deeper than did ever plummet sound
I'll drown my book."

Prospero and Miranda by William Maw Egley (around 1850)

The spectators may have felt that this is a bit hasty. After all, Prospero's usurping brother is still alive, and the Milanese might welcome a magic-wielding ruler. However, magic in Shakespeare's age was a potentially delicate subject, as it was connected to witchcraft, a burnable offense. The playwright may well have felt that Prospero's return to the world was only acceptable if he gave up being a wizard and instead became an ordinary mortal once more.

Sending Storms

Prospero's story points out another feature of wizards—they can control the weather, at least to some extent. In *The Fellowship of the Ring*, the warrior Boromir speculates that a snowstorm that is plaguing the company may be the work of Sauron. "His arm has grown long indeed," growls Gimli the dwarf, "if he can draw snow down from the North to trouble us here three hundred leagues away."

"His arm has grown long," replies Gandalf.

Tolkien's Wizards

One other significant type of wizard is that created by J.R.R. Tolkien in *The Lord of the Rings* and its associated works such as *The Silmarillion.* Tolkien reveals that there are five wizards in Middle-earth and that they were sent there by the Valar to help in the struggle against the evil of Mordor. In *The Lord of the Rings*, three of the wizards are mentioned: Gandalf the Grey (later, after his death and rebirth, Gandalf the White); Saruman the White (later Saruman of Many Colors); and Radagast the Brown. The first two are major actors in the story, whereas the third is mentioned briefly and only plays an indirect role in the events of the Third Age.

Blue Wizards

In writings that remained unpublished until his death, Tolkien said that the names of the two wizards who do not appear at all in *The Lord of the Rings* were Alatar and Pallando, and that they wore sky-blue robes.

All the wizards in Middle-earth look like old men and they age very slowly, if at all. In the sixty-some years that pass from the time of Bilbo's original adventure, recounted in *The Hobbit*, and his eleventy-first birthday, Gandalf's hair grows a bit whiter and he develops a few more wrinkles, but that's the extent of his aging. (Bilbo doesn't age much either, but for substantially different reasons.)

The wizards are Maiar, powerful spirits. (Interestingly, balrogs are fallen Maiar, which is why only Gandalf can defeat the one in Moria.) Outwardly, they appear to have only limited powers. Gandalf can start a fire, a skill that seems peculiar to him. Saruman specializes in the lore of the Elven rings, but he can also see events happening far away—though he's aided in this by use of a Palantír, a magical seeing stone. Radagast is particularly attuned to the natural world and speaks the languages of many animals.

Of the three, Saruman appears to have the least contact with Middle-earth, shutting himself up in his tower of Orthanc, whereas Gandalf and Radagast travel about a good deal. Gandalf, in particular, makes the acquaintance of many of the leaders of Middle-earth, and it is as their counselor that he plays his most important role in the struggle against Sauron.

WIZARDS AND GODS

Finally, there is another category of wizard who receives his or her power or wizardly training from the gods. Belgarath the Sorcerer, a major figure in David Eddings's epic fantasies, is trained in wizarding skills by the god Aldur, as are several others, known as Aldur's disciples. One of the benefits is apparent immortality; when he first appears in *Pawn of Prophecy*, Belgarath is 7,000 years old and widely known as the Immortal Man. The magical method Aldur teaches them is referred to as the Will and the Word, something that Belgarath passes to Garion, his descendant and the hero of the books.

Elminster, the Sage of Shadowdale, is another wizard who has a special connection to the gods—in this case to Mystra, the goddess of magic. Elminster was created by Ed Greenwood as part of the Forgotten Realms, one of the main settings for the roleplaying game Dungeons & Dragons. His magical abilities, which are considerable, are the result of being one of the Chosen of Mystra, which gives him a direct connection to her and to the magic "weave," the source of magical energy in the Forgotten Realms world of Faerûn.

Also as a Chosen of Mystra, Elminster is immortal and, if injured, can heal himself with silver fire. This has helped him out of many harrowing situations. However, when Mystra is assassinated, the result is a collapse of the Weave, an event known as the Spellplague. During the decade after Mystra's death, magic in Faerûn becomes wild and unreliable. The land itself is reshaped by vast, uncontrolled magical forces. Because of this, Elminster largely withdraws from the world.

WHERE ARE WIZARDS TAUGHT?

Actually, the question is more complicated than this. We have to ask what wizards are taught and why they have to be taught it at all.

Some wizards seem to inherit their powers through blood ties. Author Jim Butcher's Harry Dresden, for example, a wizard and private detective in modern-day Chicago, inherited his powers from his mother's side of the family. J.K. Rowling's wizards usually come from families where one or both sides of the family include wizards or witches. Significant exceptions to this exist, though. The parents of Hermione Granger, for example, are both Muggles and there's no indication of any other kind of wizarding blood in her family line. On the other hand, Argus Filch, caretaker of Hogwarts, was born to wizard parents but has no magical abilities whatsoever—the technical term for such a person is "squib." For that matter, there's no indication that Harry's grandparents were magical, yet one of their daughters, Lily, was a witch, and the other, Petunia, wasn't.

Wizards who inherit their powers must learn, through patient instruction, to control them. The witches and wizards studying at Hogwarts all have magical abilities in varying degrees, but have no idea at first how to cast spells, mix potions, or fly on broomsticks.

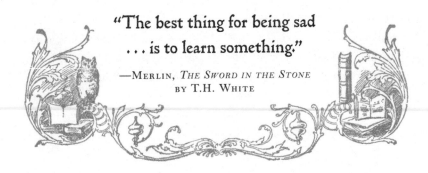

"The best thing for being sad ... is to learn something."

—MERLIN, *THE SWORD IN THE STONE*
BY T.H. WHITE

Wizards who inhabit Terry Pratchett's Discworld are in a somewhat similar position. They must attend classes at the Unseen University to master their magical powers. Rincewind, the hapless wizard who is a member of the university's faculty, has proven so inept over the years at mastering his art that it's been suggested that if he were to die the average magical quotient of everyone on the planet would actually go up a bit. Still, other students manage to make it all the way through the Unseen University and get their degrees in magic.

Among the more impressive wizard-teaching institutions are:

- Unseen University (Discworld)
- Hogwarts School of Witchcraft and Wizardry (Harry Potter series)
- College of Winterhold (Skyrim)
- Academy of Sorcery (Dragonlance)
- Palace of the Prophets (Sword of Truth series by Terry Goodkind)
- Brakebills Academy (*The Magicians* by Lev Grossman)

In some instances, wizards can be individually taught or can, sometimes, themselves be tutors. In White's *The Sword in the Stone*, Merlin undertakes young Wart's instruction by turning him into a series of animals, including a fish, a hawk, an owl, an ant, and a hedgehog. The perspective Wart gains through each of these experiences will improve his abilities as a ruler when he eventually comes to the throne under his true name, King Arthur.

THE HAZARDS OF WIZARDRY

Learning and practicing wizardry can be a terrifying and physically draining experience. Raistlin Majere's experiences in the Academy of Sorcery have left him with golden skin, and his eyes now have hour-glass-shaped pupils through which he sees the constant death and decay of everyone and everything around him. The ordeal also left him with a hacking cough and congenital weakness, and he is forced to rely for sup-port on his larger (and, some would say, stupider) brother Caramon. It is, perhaps, these physical impairments that explain why the character eventually turned to evil.

In *The Ring of Solomon*, part of Jonathan Stroud's Bartimaeus series, the magical ring held by King Solomon allows the wearer to perform impressive magic and to summon and control a mighty djinn, the Spirit of the Ring, but it comes at a cost of intense pain to the wearer.

Mary Stewart's Merlin, who can communicate with the old gods, does so in an involuntary trance, sometimes compared by critics to an epileptic fit. His prophecies, therefore, though correct and important to the rulers of Britain, incapacitate Merlin if they happen too frequently.

In all these cases, wizards survive the pain of magic because they are driven—some by ambition, some by a desire for power, others by forces they don't fully understand.

CHAPTER 2

The Power of Magic

"What is magic?

"There is the wizard's explanation . . . wizards talk about candles, circles, planets, stars, bananas, chants, runes and the importance of having at least four good meals every day."

—TERRY PRATCHETT, *LORDS AND LADIES*

 ike ice cream, wizards come in many different flavors. That is to say that there are various kinds of wizards, performing vastly diverse sorts of magic. In this chapter, we'll examine some of the strange powers of wizards and from whence those powers come.

TYPES OF MAGIC

Most wizards specialize in one or another type of magic, such as incantations, evocations, divinations, or alchemy. However, they must be familiar with all types.

Incantations

An incantation is a charm or spell created using words. The wizards in Harry Potter's world use incantations liberally, often a single word or phrase, usually in Latin. *Wingardium leviosa!* for example, is what a wizard would say in order to levitate an object. An incantation may be part of a ritual, spell, or prayer and may employ the use of physical objects, although this isn't essential.

Material Components

In Dungeons & Dragons, incantations are usually referred to as spells and often include "material components"—that is, objects of some kind. These are as varied as a pinch of dirt taken from a graveyard or a silver dagger. D&D spells are organized by "level." The higher the level, the more complex the spell and the more experienced the wizard must be to cast it.

In Marian Cockrell's delightful young-adult fantasy novel *Shadow Castle*, material components for a wizard's spell include a pair of rainbows that keep bumping into one another. Some wizards make use of objects in their spells, but for others, an incantation is simply a matter of putting forth one's will. Such is the case with David Eddings's Belgarath. As mentioned in the previous chapter, Belgarath uses a method called the Will and the Word to cast his incantations. This consists of envisioning the Word that names the object to be affected and drawing upon a kind of universal Will or power to create the spell. Mastering the skills of spellcasting in Eddings's universe takes a long time, and Belgarath, under the tutelage of the god Aldur, spends decades trying to create the simplest of magics. Finally, out of frustration more than anything else, he tries to move a massive boulder and succeeds without being entirely conscious of what he is doing. He then spends several thousand more years mastering and controlling this power.

Incantations are not to be undertaken by those without experience in such things or who do not possess the proper equipment. In *Harry Potter and the Prisoner of Azkaban*, Ron Weasley, angered beyond endurance by the bully Draco Malfoy, hurls a slug-eating spell at him. Unfortunately, because Ron's wand has been damaged, the spell backfires, and slugs come pouring out of Ron's own mouth.

The words that accompany a spell are essential to producing the effect the wizard wants. Some spells don't require words; others depend heavily upon them. In John Boorman's 1981 film *Excalibur*, Merlin makes use of "the Charm of Making" and chants words meant to be some variant of a Celtic language.

The Charm of Making

It's been suggested that the words Merlin uses in *Excalibur* are derived from Old Irish:

Anál nathrach,
orth' bháis's bethad,
do chél dénmha

This Old Irish incantation would translate roughly into English as:

Serpent's breath,
charm of death and life,
thy omen of making.

Boorman himself has never said where the words come from.

Such words, as mentioned previously, are essential to the wizards of J.K. Rowling's Harry Potter stories. The most important incantation—at any rate, the most feared—is the Killing Curse. The wizard raises his wand, points it at the subject, and utters the words, *Avada Kedavra.* The subject of the curse dies immediately.

Alert readers probably notice a close connection between the words of the Killing Curse and the familiar magical word *Abracadabra*. No one quite knows where the latter comes from; some speculate that it's Aramaic for "I create as I speak." It first appears in the third century A.D. in a medical book written by Quintus Serenus Sammonicus. Noted magicians once used it, but now it's largely used by stage magicians and no longer taken seriously as an incantation.

EVOCATIONS

To evoke is to call or summon a spirit, demon, or god. It's a practice deeply rooted in Western mystery schools such as the Rites of Dionysus or the Eleusinian Mysteries of Ancient Greece. A wizard often stands within a magic circle or pentagram (a five-sided star) and summons a being, compelling it by the terms of the evocation to obey the wizard's commands.

"I hate to break this to you, but as a rule, wizards are nasty people. They're powerful, capricious, ruthless, egotistical, used to getting their own way. That's being kind. "

—JASON HALEY, *THE WIZARD HEIR* BY CINDA WILLIAMS CHIMA

As one can imagine, this sort of thing can get badly out of hand. In Jonathan Stroud's Bartimaeus novels, wizards summon demons to perform chores for them. However, the demons are constrained only by the precise words of the spell. If the wizard mispronounces a word or steps out of his circle of protection, the demon is released from the spell, usually with very unpleasant results for the magician.

Players of the collectible card game Magic: The Gathering are familiar with evocations, as this is one of the main tactics in the game. Two players, pretending to be rival magicians, use cards from their decks to summon creatures. Once summoned, the creatures can attack the player's opponent or block her spells or creatures from attacking him.

The Cost of Summoning

Magic: The Gathering players are able to summon creatures by using magic, known in the game as "mana." When a creature is summoned by the wizard, it is considered to have "summoning sickness" and can only be used on the player's next turn.

At the end, when the summoned creature—be it demon or god or spirit—has done its work, the wizard must also know the proper way to dismiss it. This allows it to return to the plane of existence from which it was called.

Necromancy

Necromancy, or raising people (and other beings) from the dead, is not a skill all wizards have, though it's obviously a very useful one to possess.

H.P. Lovecraft, the American horror and supernatural writer, dealt with this subject in his 1927 novella *The Case of Charles Dexter Ward*. In this story, a young man living in Providence, Rhode Island, is drawn into the evil plans of a distant ancestor to gather the "essential Saltes" of various prominent thinkers from all ages of humankind and resurrect them so they can be tortured and their knowledge drained. Eventually the ancestor, Joseph Curwen, whom Ward has also raised from the dead, murders Ward and takes his place. The eldritch wizard is stopped by the timely intervention of the Wards' family doctor, who detects the plot and casts his own spell to dissolve Curwen's body back into dust.

The term "necromancer" itself has become somewhat debased, and authors and filmmakers occasionally use it in place of "wizard." In J.R.R. Tolkien's *The Hobbit*, for example, Sauron is referred to as the Necromancer, though there's no suggestion that he resurrects anyone in pursuance of his plans to conquer Middle-earth.

Not everyone who brings people back from the dead is necessarily a necromancer. The Norse god Odin, for example, brings a prophetess back from the dead to show him the future. In the Bible, Jesus resurrects Lazarus (and several others). However, neither Odin nor Jesus could be described as a necromancer, since they don't rely upon spells or other forms of magic to achieve this end.

DIVINATION

Probably as a result of the ridiculous divination teacher in the Harry Potter books, this aspect of magic has gotten a bit of a bad reputation. That's unfortunate, because it is an important part of a wizard's skill: the ability to communicate with otherworldly forces and to read the future.

As we saw in the previous chapter, Merlin was considered an important prophet, and his predictions of the future shaped Arthur's policies. However, the tradition of soothsaying is far older than Merlin.

For instance, we read in the Bible that when the prophet Samuel died, King Saul banished from the kingdom "those that had familiar spirits, and the wizards." Unfortunately, the Philistines massed on the border of the kingdom and Saul, being unable to get advice from the Lord, sent for a woman, sometimes referred to as the witch of Endor, who had a familiar (that is, a magical assistant, often in the form of an animal) and who was able to raise the prophet from the dead. Unfortunately, this didn't do Saul much good, as Samuel prophesied that Saul would be defeated in battle and would join Samuel in the afterlife. Following his defeat by the Philistines, Saul committed suicide, fulfilling Samuel's prophecy from beyond the grave.

In Ancient Greece, people sought guidance from oracles. The most famous of these was the Oracle at Delphi on Mount Parnassus. There, a priestess (perhaps overcome by volcanic fumes rising from the earth) went into a trance and offered divine advice. As time went by, the function of the priestess or priest was gradually taken over by wizards, who interpreted signs and sought to connect through their powers with the gods to know the future.

"We are merely the stars'
tennis-balls, struck and banded
Which way please them."

—Bosola,
THE DUCHESS OF MALFI
BY JOHN WEBSTER

Astrology

One popular form of divination among wizards and others has been astrology, or the interpretation of the positions and movements of the heavenly bodies through the skies and how these relate to life on earth. The practice dates back to at least 1000 B.C. (when it was largely practiced by Islamic scholars) and was widely used in Europe during the Renaissance. It's noteworthy that in the Harry Potter books, Harry and his friends spend time studying the heavens and interpreting various astrological patterns. It's also important to keep in mind that many magical spells work better when the stars, sun, moon, and planets are in particular configurations.

Today, among non-wizarding folk, astrology is a familiar feature of the cultural landscape. Newspapers print horoscopes, and a professional stargazer will draw up a personalized one for you. Just as alchemy is considered a precursor of chemistry, so astrology is an ancestor of modern astronomy.

Astrology proposes that events are affected by the positions of the heavenly bodies. Of particular importance, in terms of your personality

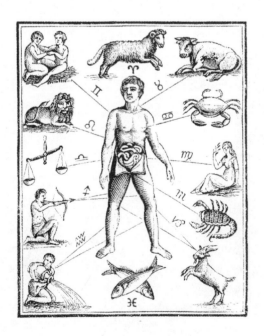

and life potential, is the zodiac sign in which the sun was positioned when you were born. The signs are:

◆ Aries	◆ Leo	◆ Sagittarius
◆ Taurus	◆ Virgo	◆ Capricorn
◆ Gemini	◆ Libra	◆ Aquarius
◆ Cancer	◆ Scorpio	◆ Pisces

Your "sun sign," however, is only a part of a much larger and more complex picture.

Wizards are adept at studying the skies and drawing up birth charts. John Dee (c. 1527–1608), a figure in the court of Elizabeth I of England, was a noted astrologer and used his knowledge of cosmic matters to advise his royal mistress, the queen.

Divination Through Dreams

Another important method of divination is through the interpretation of dreams. Wizards are skilled both in telling others the meaning of their dreams and in entering dreamlike trances in which they can communicate with other planes of existence. In literature, this tradition is particularly strong among Celtic magic users. In the ancient ritual of *tarbh feis*, a magician drank broth made from a freshly killed bull or ate the flesh, then wrapped himself in the bull's hide and waited to be overtaken by a vision (the Scottish version of this was called the *taghairm*). Animal sacrifice is not normally a part of Celtic or most other forms of magic today.

Mary Stewart's Merlin makes his prophecies as a result of going into dreamlike states (as mentioned earlier, more like seizures). In these conditions, he is able to speak with the voice of the Old Gods, predicting the future of England and telling listeners what is happening in a far distant part of the country.

THE TAROT DECK

Among the most powerful predictive tools used by wizards (and today by many other people) is the Tarot. These cards probably originated in fifteenth-century Italy and evolved over the next few centuries. According to tradition, they are based on the wisdom of ancient Egypt as well as, possibly, the mystical Kabbalah of the Jewish faith.

A typical deck contains seventy-eight cards—twenty-two constitute the Major Arcana and fifty-six comprise the Minor Arcana. The user shuffles the cards and lays them out in an established pattern (you can learn many of the standard Tarot spreads online or from a basic book on Tarot readings). The wizard or other reader will then interpret the cards, both in terms of which cards appear and their order and relationship to one another within the spread.

The Magician

One particularly significant Tarot card is the Magician. This card, which is part of the Major Arcana, depicts the magician holding aloft a wand. His other hand points toward the earth, symbolizing the link between the worlds above and below. Above his head is the symbol for infinity. He wears a belt that sometimes takes the form of a snake biting its tail (the ourobouros), a symbol also used in alchemy to denote wholeness.

The Magician card signifies the power of the universe, provided that we have the wisdom to absorb and understand it. It shows that reality and illusion are, in fact, two sides of the same coin, and to understand them we must use both our intuitive and intellectual powers. The card shows us the potential of our creative abilities and our power to affect the universe around us.

In Chapter 1 you learned of various kinds of wizards, often defined by the branch of wizardry with which they concern themselves (for example, astrologers study astrology, alchemists practice alchemy, and so on). Now let's take a closer look at some of these types and see how they're distinct from one another.

Magus

This word has ancient roots and was used at one time to refer to followers of the religious leader Zoroaster. The three kings from the East who attended the birth of Jesus, as described in the Gospel of Matthew, are referred to as the Three Magi. However, this doesn't necessarily mean they were wizards; in this context the word seems to mean "wise men." It is, of course, the root word of "magic," "mage," and "magician."

Keeping this in mind, the magus is most often a wizard who is noted for his wisdom and ability to give good counsel, as well as for his magical abilities. Gandalf, with his long, white beard, is one such wizard who gives the impression of great age and experience. Elminster of Shadowdale is another.

John Fowles's The Magus

In 1965, the postmodern author John Fowles (1926–2005) published a novel, *The Magus*, that stirred much debate in literary circles. The novel tells the story of a young Englishman, Nicholas Urfe, who goes to live on a small Greek island. There he meets the mysterious Maurice Conchis, whom he befriends. Gradually, Urfe becomes aware that there is something sinister about Conchis; the older man seems to be playing an elaborate game with him, drawing him into a world in which illusion and reality become indistinguishable. More and more, Urfe begins to realize that the stories about Conchis's past life (including his collaboration with the Nazis in World War II) are, in fact, about Urfe's own life and give him a new means of seeing.

Keepers of Lore

Magi are repositories of lore. Gandalf, in the *The Lord of the Rings*, has lived through three ages of Middle-earth (though he is not the oldest living thing in Middle-earth) and in those thousands of years he has absorbed the stories of all its peoples. This includes even the hobbits, of whom virtually everyone else in Middle-earth is unaware; as Gandalf remarks, "Among the Wise, I am the only one that goes in for hobbit-lore." This knowledge proves crucial when the fate of Middle-earth hangs in the balance and Gandalf entrusts the task of destroying the Ring of Power to a hobbit.

How Much Magic Is Enough?

Fans of *The Lord of the Rings* may be surprised to realize that for a wizard Gandalf really doesn't do much magic in the course of the story. His main ability is to manipulate fire, which he does on several occasions—starting a fire in the snowstorm on the slopes of Mount Caradhras, fighting off the wolf attack in Hollin, and a few other occasions. His staff is capable of shedding light, as it does in Moria, and he uses it in some way to render Wormtongue harmless. Apart from that, his role is largely as a counselor: to Aragorn, to Théoden, and to Denethor (though the latter rejects his advice with attendant bad consequences).

SORCERER

A magus is a source of wisdom and lore, whereas in games and literature a sorcerer is usually a figure of action. Pictures of sorcerers tend to show them with swirling robes, lightning crackling from their fingertips as they cast spells, while storm clouds pile in the background and rain lashes the ground.

Sorcerers are often thought of as evil, but this is not necessarily the case. Nonetheless, in stories and lore they are usually depicted as darker and more forbidding than magi.

Sorcerers and Shapeshifters

It should be noted that in many traditions, sorcerers have many other abilities. For instance, in Native American folklore, sorcerers are noted shapeshifters who can move between the physical and nonphysical worlds, work with spirits, alter their appearances, and split their energies so they can send their etheric "doubles" to appear in various places at once. It should also be said that the words "sorcerer," "wizard," "magician," and "shaman" are often used interchangeably in folklore.

The Sorcerer's Apprentice

Among the best-known sorcerers is the one, who, having important business elsewhere, tells his apprentice to perform a series of household chores, including fetching water. Tired of this menial labor, the apprentice, who has been carefully watching how his master casts spells, enchants a broom to do the work for him. Unfortunately, the apprentice has no idea how to make the broom *stop* fetching water, and the floor is soon flooded. Grabbing a handy ax, the apprentice splits the broom in half, but now both halves continue to carry water from the well to the overflowing chamber.

Happily, the sorcerer returns just in time to break the spell and end the disaster. The implied lesson of the story is not to meddle with forces you can't control.

The tale was first told in a 1797 poem by the German writer Johann Wolfgang von Goethe. However, the form in which most people know it is as part of the Disney animated film *Fantasia* (1940). The action, which stars Mickey Mouse as the apprentice, is based on the Goethe poem and accompanied by the music of Beethoven, Stravinsky, Ponchielli, and Schubert. In the movie, the broom multiplies again and again. The magician returns, halts the disaster, and glares at Mickey, who picks up the bucket, sighs, and is driven from the room with a smack from the sorcerer.

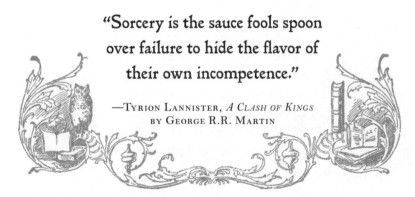

> ## "Sorcery is the sauce fools spoon over failure to hide the flavor of their own incompetence."
>
> —TYRION LANNISTER, *A CLASH OF KINGS* BY GEORGE R.R. MARTIN

Atlantes

Another notable sorcerer was Atlantes, an African enchanter and a character in the rambling Renaissance epic poem *Orlando Furioso*. The poem, first published in 1532, was written by an Italian, Ludovico Ariosto, and is set in the age of Charlemagne (that is, the late eighth and early ninth centuries). The hero is Orlando, one of Charlemagne's knights, who is in love with the beautiful Angelica, a pagan princess. She, however, falls in love with a Moorish knight and runs off with him to the East, and Orlando, in a rage, goes on a killing spree through Europe and Asia.

Meanwhile, a Saracen knight named Ruggiero finds himself in a somewhat parallel situation, having fallen in love with a Christian, Bradamante. Atlantes is Ruggiero's foster father, a powerful wizard who does not want his son killed in the wars and therefore devises various diversions to hold his attention. Atlantes operates as we're accustomed to seeing magic users do.

Atlantes from the threshold, graved by skill,
With characters and wondrous signs, upturned
A virtuous stone, where, underneath the sill,
Pots, with perpetual fire and secret, burned.
The enchanter breaks them; and at once the hill
To an inhospitable rock is turned.

Atlantes builds a huge castle filled with illusions that he hopes will divert his foster son, because he is convinced Ruggiero will be captured by Charlemagne's forces and converted to Christianity. Eventually, the knight is freed by Bradamante and does, indeed, convert, whereupon he marries his rescuer.

The Crimson King

Both Atlantes and the unnamed sorcerer in *The Sorcerer's Apprentice* might be said to be at least not evil, if not actually good. However, Stephen King's creation, the Crimson King, is unabashedly on the side of the forces of darkness. The main antagonist in King's novel cycle The Dark Tower, he is also a force behind the scenes in King's *The Stand*, *Insomnia*, and *Black House*, written by King and Peter Straub.

The Crimson King lives in a state apart from our reality; his intention in The Dark Tower is to bring down the tower, which holds the universes together, so he can rule over the resulting chaos. He appears in many different forms—an old man with glowing red eyes, a good-looking blond man—but we have no clue as to what his real form is. Generally, King seems to identify the Crimson King with Satan, though this isn't made explicit.

ALCHEMISTS

As mentioned earlier, alchemy has a long history. The origins of the name are obscure, although the "al" would seem to indicate an Arabic provenance. It may possibly come from "al-Khem"; *Khem* was the Arabic word for Egypt, which could mean that the beginnings of alchemy can be traced to that time-shrouded land.

In ancient Greece, philosophers such as Thales and Anaximander believed that all the objects we see around us were made of some common "stuff" and with the right processes could be reduced to that stuff. In the case of Thales, this stuff was water. Anaximander believed it was a kind of undifferentiated primordial mass. Alchemy proceeds from the same general idea: If everything is made of essentially the same material, it should be possible to transmute one type of metal into another if only we can find the right process to do so.

To this end, they collected masses of obscure materials and set about boiling, dissolving, reducing, and reconstituting them. They started from Aristotle's observation that the world is composed of four elements: earth, air, water, and fire. Some interaction of these elements, they were convinced, would produce the result they were looking for. Their efforts ended in failure, but along the way they laid the foundations of modern chemistry.

Many wizards have some background in alchemy. Among Harry Potter's classes at Hogwarts is Potions. This is not strictly devoted to alchemy but includes large numbers of alchemical factors. Certainly it involves a lot of stirring and dissolving and occasional explosions.

Among the best-known, real-life alchemists are:

- Al-Razi (c. 866–c. 925)
- Alain de Lille (c. 1115–c. 1202)
- Albertus Magnus (1193–1280)

- ◆ Roger Bacon (c. 1213–1294)
- ◆ Ramon Llull (c. 1232–1315)
- ◆ Johann Georg Faust (c. 1480–1540)
- ◆ Heinrich Cornelius Agrippa (1486–1535)
- ◆ Paracelsus (1493–1541)
- ◆ Nicholas Flamel (15th century)
- ◆ John Dee (1527–1609?)
- ◆ Tycho Brahe (1546–1601)
- ◆ Claude Adrien Helvétius (1715–1771)
- ◆ Robert Boyle (1627–1691)
- ◆ Isaac Newton (1642–1727)
- ◆ Conte Allesandro di Cagliostro (1743–1795)
- ◆ Count St. Germain (1712–1784)

The Englishman Roger Bacon (c. 1213–1294), a polymath, made contributions to both science and philosophy. Later scholars were amazed at the range of his learning and could only attribute it to magical powers that he must have had at his command. Bacon was suggested as the author of the mysterious *Voynich Manuscript*, a book written in code that has never been broken but that seems to deal with alchemical and possibly magical matters. Bacon also wrote the key alchemical text *Speculum Alchemiae*, translated as *The Mirror of Alchemy*.

One of the principles of alchemy was that the more rare and precious a substance, the greater its potential to give rise to the Philosopher's Stone. Some alchemists experimented with using gold itself as a medicine. Paracelsus, for instance, discovered that gold could be used to treat epileptic fits. (Homeopaths today still use gold (arum) to treat ailments.)

This fact also illustrates the close connections that often formed in the Middle Ages between alchemists and doctors. This is characteristic of wizards in myth as well; their occult abilities often made them useful healers. Mary Stewart's Merlin, for example, is called to court from his hermetic life when King Uther Pendragon becomes ill. Merlin alone, the nobility believes, can save the great king from death (and, in fact, it proves so).

The Philosopher's Stone

It's been mentioned that one of the goals of alchemists is to find the Philosopher's Stone. In some accounts, this is an actual stone or at least a real substance—possibly a liquid contained within a stone, a liquid that proves to have magical properties such as conferring eternal life. For other alchemists, the Philosopher's Stone is an abstract concept. The word "philosopher" means "seeker of wisdom," so the Stone was representative of this search.

Some even identified the Philosopher's Stone with the Holy Grail of Arthurian legend. The Stone is thus a cup, the one Christ drank from at the Last Supper and the cup that was used to catch his blood when he was pierced by a Roman spear while on the Cross.

The most important alchemical work was the *Tabula Smaragdina* (sometimes called the *Emerald Tablet*). It is said to have been written by Hermes Trismegistus—the last name translates roughly as "thrice great"—the Egyptian god of wisdom and a kind of patron saint of alchemy. His writings were brought to the West by Miriam, sister of Moses. The *Tabula Smaragdina* was part of a batch of writings called the Corpus Hermeticum that formed the basis for a long magical tradition in Western Europe, one that has lasted to the present day.

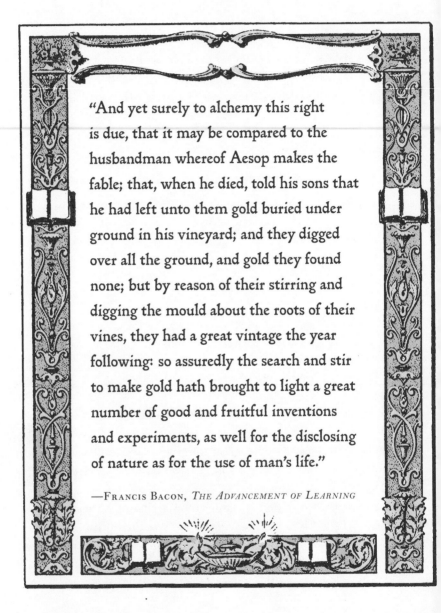

"And yet surely to alchemy this right is due, that it may be compared to the husbandman whereof Aesop makes the fable; that, when he died, told his sons that he had left unto them gold buried under ground in his vineyard; and they digged over all the ground, and gold they found none; but by reason of their stirring and digging the mould about the roots of their vines, they had a great vintage the year following: so assuredly the search and stir to make gold hath brought to light a great number of good and fruitful inventions and experiments, as well for the disclosing of nature as for the use of man's life."

—FRANCIS BACON, *THE ADVANCEMENT OF LEARNING*

SHAMANS

Shamanism has an extensive tradition throughout the world. Although the term was once applied exclusively to magicians among the Turks and Mongols, it gradually spread west to Europe. Scholars have also found it in religious practices in Africa and throughout Asia, as well as North and South America.

A shaman is a wizard who is able to go into a trance or state of altered consciousness and, in that state, see things that are hidden from ordinary mortals. Shamans are also noted for their ability to move between the worlds and to shapeshift, often into animals or birds. The great Romanian historian of religion, Mircea Eliade, says:

> "Of course, the shaman is also a magician and medicine man; he is believed to cure, like all doctors, and to perform miracles . . . But beyond this . . . he may also be priest, mystic, and poet."

Just as the magus is often depicted as wearing robes and a long beard, so the shaman may don a costume that proclaims his calling. The clothing varies a bit from culture to culture, but it often includes:

* A cloak made of animal hide. Northern European shamans use the skin of reindeer. Native American shamans in the southwestern United States may wear the skins of deer, bear, wolves, or other animals from which they seek assistance.
* Feathers, symbolizing the ability of the shaman's spirit to take flight. Many shamans wear costumes or masks that resemble a bird. Mongol shamans,

for instance, have wings on their shoulders. Native American shamans may don the feathers of eagles or other birds.

- ◆ Bells, rattles, or other objects that will make noise and frighten
  away evil spirits.
- ◆ Some shamans wear masks, to attract or repel spirits, or for other
  purposes.

Shamans often play drums in conjunction with their magical rituals.
The wood of the drum may come from a tree that, to the shaman, symbolizes the World Tree that grows at the heart of the world. Some shamans go into the forest and, in a mystical trance, choose the right tree.
Others look for trees struck by lightning. Shamans often offer sacrifices
to trees to thank them for their wood; in parts of Siberia, this might
mean dabbing the tree with a mixture of blood and vodka.

Once in a trance, shamans can enter other worlds, which enables
them to see both the future and the present. Frequently, they travel
through these worlds accompanied by a familiar spirit, often, but not
always, in the form of an animal. This animal will probably be reflected
in the shaman's costume.

Familiars

Familiars, or animal helpers
of witches and wizards, are widespread in magical lore and are not
confined to shamans. In the world
of Harry Potter, the students at
Hogwarts are encouraged to bring
animals to school; Harry, as readers know, brings his owl, Hedwig,
whereas Ron brings the family rat,

Scabbers (who is not all he seems), and Hermione acquires the grumpy, squashed-faced cat, Crookshanks.

T.H. White's Merlin has an owl, Archimedes, who is prone to offer Wart advice different from his master's. At one point, Merlin changes Wart into an owl so he can experience things from the bird's point of view. The owl is a common wizarding companion, as it represents wisdom through its association with Athena, the Greek goddess of wisdom.

Occasionally, wizards have demons or other spirits as familiars. In the world of Philip Pullman's His Dark Materials trilogy, daemons are a form of human souls and as such accompany their masters.

Familiars in Space

In the original series of the television show *Star Trek*, Robert Bloch (author of *Psycho*, made famous by the Hitchcock film of the same name) wrote a Halloween episode in which the starship *Enterprise* encounters a mysterious robed man named Korob and his black cat familiar.

The cat, it develops, can also take the form of a beautiful woman named Sylvia. She and Korob are explorers from another galaxy and have the power to transmute and control matter. When she dangles a model of the *Enterprise* above a lit candle, the actual ship's hull rises in temperature.

In the end, Captain Kirk succeeds in destroying the transmuter, killing Korob and Sylvia.

Mr. Spock: There are ancient Earth legends about wizards and their familiars.
Dr. McCoy: Familiars?
Mr. Spock: Demons in animal form sent by Satan to serve the wizard.
Captain James T. Kirk: Superstition.
Mr. Spock: I do not create the legend, Captain. I merely report it.

WIZARDS' DWELLING PLACES

Although some wizards, such as twenty-first-century magic user Harry Dresden, live in ordinary surroundings, most wizards have a special place to which they can retreat. In myths and popular stories, this is either a tower or a cave.

Isengard

In Tolkien's Middle-earth, Saruman the White is the only one of the five wizards to make himself a permanent home. He chooses the ancient tower of Orthanc, set in the middle of the fortress of Isengard. This makes his position invulnerable to attack—or so he thinks.

Isengard consists of a large rock ring (called the Ring of Isengard) that was pierced by a gate, heavily guarded in Saruman's time. When Saruman turned to evil during the Third Age, due to the temptation of the Ring of Power, he turned Isengard into a place of evil and used it to breed a new kind of orc. The fortress was attacked by ents during the War of the Ring, who tore down the rock and the gates and diverted the River Isen to flood the entire ring.

At the center of this ring, stood the tower of Orthanc where Saruman dwelt. Although built by mortal men, some magic was used in its construction, because it could not be harmed, even by the ents, who are the strongest living creatures in Middle-earth. It consisted of four large columns that joined together and rose for 500 feet. At the summit they divided into four sharp-pointed towers, and between them was a small space with runes and magical symbols engraved into the rock. It was in this space that Saruman imprisoned Gandalf briefly, the latter escaping only with the aid of the eagles.

The Crystal Cave

Mary Stewart's novel *The Crystal Cave* puts the enchanter Merlin in a cave in Wales. The cave is magical, with a soft wind that blows through it and occasionally makes music from the strings of Merlin's harp. Stewart's Merlin is based largely on druidic traditions and is more a seer than an active mover in the world's affairs. He remains in his cave for years, leaving only to arrange for Arthur to be fostered with Sir Ector until he comes of age to be king.

In John Boorman's film *Excalibur*, Merlin's cave, it is suggested, is actually beneath Arthur's palace at Camelot. There, Merlin can awaken the Dragon (a symbol of Britain) and do magic, using the dragon's breath. The television show *Merlin*, starring Colin Morgan, uses a somewhat similar idea but with the added twist that the cave contains a real dragon, imprisoned there. The dragon talks to young Merlin occasionally, telling him that he must protect Arthur. At the end of the second season, Merlin releases the dragon, which promptly wreaks vengeance on Camelot for having imprisoned it.

CHAPTER 3

A Wizard's Equipment

"It is . . . no argument against ceremonial magic to say that it is 'absurd' to try to raise a thunderstorm by beating a drum; it is not even fair to say that you have tried the experiment, found it would not work, and so perceived it to be 'impossible.' You might as well claim that, as you had taken paint and canvas, and not produced a Rembrandt, it was evident that the pictures attributed to his painting were really produced in quite a different way."

—*THE MOONCHILD* BY ALEISTER CROWLEY

hortly after discovering that he's a wizard, Harry Potter must go shopping for school supplies. Because he's enrolled in Hogwarts School of Witchcraft and Wizardry, these supplies entail a bit more than pens, pencils, and notebooks. Harry must purchase a wand, a cauldron, spellbooks, a set of wizard robes, quills and ink, and much more.

A wizard's basic equipment isn't necessarily all that complicated. It depends on the circumstances. An established wizard with a laboratory will have a good deal more equipment than a hedge wizard who travels from town to town and by necessity must bring along only what he can carry. Still, there are some things virtually every legendary wizard needs.

THE WAND OR STAFF

"The wand chooses the wizard." So says the mysterious Mr. Ollivander in *Harry Potter and the Sorcerer's Stone*. This isn't true in the world of real magic and wizardry, but it makes for an entertaining scene in the Potter story. The wand or staff carried by a wizard is among the most personal of her or his possessions.

The tradition of wands is very old, going back at least to ancient Greece. The poet Homer in *The Odyssey* recounts that Circe used a silver wand to transform Odysseus's men into swine. Some scholars have theorized that the wand and especially the wizard's staff are related to the image of the World Tree (mentioned in Chapter 2). Thus the wand or staff signifies that the wizard is in touch with the mystic center of the world and is able to draw upon its magical powers.

A Symbol

The wand can also be a symbol of masculine energy, as well as a symbol of the fire element. A magician uses both masculine and feminine forces in spellwork, as well as the four elements—earth, air, fire, and water—and his or her tools represent these elements.

That the wand is a powerful weapon is shown by C.S. Lewis's White Witch, the main villain in *The Lion, the Witch, and the Wardrobe.* She uses her wand to transform people and animals into stone. In the last battle with her, Edmund Pevensie swings his sword not at her but at the wand, breaking it and destroying its magical power. Without it, the witch is an ordinary mortal and is slain by the lion king Aslan at the conclusion of the battle.

Gandalf uses his staff to start fires and shed light, and as already mentioned is able to summon lightning to blast a traitor into unconsciousness in *The Two Towers.* The wizard's staff in Tolkien's world is both a source and a symbol of his power; when Gandalf confronts Saruman in the ruins of Isengard and casts him from the White Council, he declares, "Saruman, your staff is broken." And, in fact, Saruman's staff splits and the top of it falls at Gandalf's feet. Although Saruman still possesses the seductive power of his voice, he has lost the ability to call on his other magics, and he is doomed until almost the end of the story to wander Middle-earth, ragged and friendless.

Khelben Arunsun, magical ruler of the city of Waterdeep in the Forgotten Realms, a world in the Dungeons & Dragons universe, was actually identified by his staff, the famous "blackstaff." Unlike his fellow wizard Elminster, Khelben preferred to keep people off balance, and he was able to do so with impressive magical displays from his staff. Upon his death in the Realms year 1374 (the events of which are described in Steven Schend's novel *Blackstaff*), Khelben's staff was passed to his apprentice Tsarra, who continues to wield its power.

THE CAULDRON

At Hogwarts, cauldrons are most often used in Professor Snape's Potions classes, as students brew up a potpourri of magic mixes. In fact, wizards and witches sometimes use cauldrons for precisely this purpose.

In Shakespeare's *Macbeth*, the three witches who foretell Macbeth's destiny gather again at the beginning of Act IV to meet with him and offer further prophecies. Before he arrives, they brew a magic spell in their cauldron:

> "Round about the caldron go;
> In the poison'd entrails throw.
> Toad, that under cold stone,
> Days and nights has thirty-one
> Swelter'd venom sleeping got,
> Boil thou first i' the charmed pot!"

The spell enables them to tell Macbeth that he will not be defeated in battle until "Great Birnam wood to high Dunsinane hill shall come against him."

MACBETH.

Pentagrams and Pentacles

One of a magician's most important tools, the pentagram is a five-sided star, usually with a circle around it. It serves as a symbol of protection. It can be drawn on paper, wood, metal, fabric, on the ground, or in the air as part of a spell or ritual. Many wizards and witches wear pentagrams as jewelry. You can hang one on your front door or from your car's rearview mirror to keep you safe.

A pentacle is often a tile, plate, trivet, or other object decorated with a five-pointed star that's usually surrounded by a circle. A wizard or witch might place this object on her altar to hold things, such as food, that will be used in a ritual. Both the pentagram and pentacle represent the element of earth.

"The manner of constructing circles is not always one and the same. It is customary to change it according to the kind of spirits which are to be evoked, and the places, seasons, days, and hours; because in setting up a circle is it necessary to take into consideration at what time of year, on which day, and in which hour you are making it: which spirits you want to summon, the star and region over which they reside: in which particular tasks they carry out."

—Pietro d'Abano, *Heptameron*

Swords and Athames

Among the most important tools used by ritual magicians are swords and athames. In Chapter Four we'll discuss one of the most famous of all legendary swords, King Arthur's Excalibur. Here, it's sufficient to remark that swords and daggers (called athames) represent the element of air (in the Tarot deck, the suit of Swords is associated with air).

Athames, sacred daggers, have been used by wizards in rituals going back to the thirteenth century. In magic, they are used to clear away negative forces that might interfere with the wizard's spell. Although in modern wizardry and witchcraft the athame is never used to cause physical harm to a person, daggers and swords of legend have not always been so kind. We can remember that Gandalf the Grey carried the sword Glamdring with which he opposed the balrog in the Mines of Moria. The sword of Godric Gryffindor was key to Harry Potter's victory over Voldemort. And in David Eddings's Belgariad series, it is the mystical sword of the Rivan King that marks out young Garion as the heir to the throne of the West.

The four Elements

Four of the wizard's primary tools, the chalice or cauldron, the wand, the athame, and the pentagram, correspond to the four elements: water, fire, air, and earth. The pentagram's five star points represent the human body: head, arms, and legs.

CLOTHING

Clothing in the legendary wizarding world largely consists of robes. They make for easy movement when casting spells and are low maintenance. In some instances, the color of the robe determines the wizard's status. For example, the world of Dragonlance has three types of wizards: white robes, red robes, and black robes.

- White robes are wizards who use their magical powers for healing and to advance magical knowledge. They are supporters of the forces of good.
- Red-robed wizards focus their powers on illusion and transmutation. In the conflict between good and evil, they are neutral.

- Black robes, not surprisingly, are supporters of evil. In this capacity they master the arts of necromancy and enchantment, which in the Dragonlance world are generally evil.

Wizards of Tolkien's Middle-earth wear different colored robes to some degree as an indication of status. Saruman wore a white robe before his fall, and was the leader of the White Council, a gathering of the wizards and other powerful folk of Middle-earth. When Saruman betrayed the opponents of Sauron, his staff was broken and Gandalf assumed the white robes and changed from Gandalf the Grey to Gandalf the White. Radagast, presumably, remained Radagast the Brown.

In other settings, the color of one's robe is unimportant—all the wizards at Hogwarts wear black robes.

"Do you know how wizards like to be buried?"

"Yes!"

"Well, how?"

Granny Weatherwax paused at the bottom of the stairs.

"Reluctantly."

—TERRY PRACHETT, *EQUAL RITES*

Not all wizards wear robes, of course. In The Dresden Files series, Harry Dresden, the only wizard listed in the Chicago phone book, wears a leather duster, which gives him a stylish look as a private investigator. There's no indication that historical figures such as John Dee, Paracelsus, or Aleister Crowley wore robes (although Crowley may have done so on ceremonial occasions).

Wizard robes may be decorated with arcane symbols, such as alchemical or astrological glyphs that convey occult ideas or information. In lore and fantasy, the symbols and formulae may inspire awe or serve as mnemonics for the wearers. Pointed hats are optional.

MISCELLANY

Many wizards are also musicians; Mary Stewart's Merlin, for instance, plays the harp and travels about Britain disguised as a bard. A harp or flute is easy to carry and helpful sometimes as an accompaniment to a spell. This is particularly true if the instrument is magical in some way.

Wizards also sometimes use crystal balls or other scrying devices to see beyond what the human eye can perceive. Gandalf, briefly, possessed a Palantír, one of the seven seeing stones.

Runes

We've already mentioned the arcane symbols used by wizards, many of them drawn from astrology and alchemy. Many wizards made use of an additional form of writing: runes.

Runes were created by the Scandinavian people—some said the god Odin brought them to his followers. When the Vikings began their systematic raiding in northern England during the eighth and ninth centuries, runic writings began to show up all over the north of Britain. From there, runes spread to the Continent, where they were carried by the Vikings very far indeed. Visitors today to the great shrine of Hagia Sophia in Istanbul can see runic symbols scrawled on a balcony rail by long-ago Viking visitors. The Vikings carried their runes down the rivers of Russia, through the Mediterranean to southern Italy, and across the English Channel to Normandy (so named as the home of the "Northmen").

Runes were a form of writing, but for wizards they had an added significance; each rune is named for an animal, object, condition, or deity. For example, the rune Berkana, which looks like our letter B, symbolizes a birch tree and thus represents growth.

Wizards often used runes to write spells and spellbooks. In crafting *The Lord of the Rings*, J.R.R. Tolkien used them as the language of the dwarves. Today, magic users employ them as writing in crystals, amulets, and other magical objects.

The future in the Crystal

Many wizards have used crystal balls or other forms of crystal to see the future—or at least visions of events occurring far away. John Dee, court magician to Elizabeth I, was noted for his work with crystals. The Wicked Witch of the West in the film version of L. Frank Baum's *The Wonderful Wizard of Oz* used a crystal ball to track the progress of Dorothy and her friends toward the Emerald City. Even Shakespeare's Prospero is sometimes depicted with a crystal ball as he summons the tempest that strands his brother on the island with him.

Spellbooks

Among the most important elements of a wizard's equipment are his spellbooks. These are sometimes written by him, but more frequently contain the carefully assembled lore, spells, and magical practices of many years' effort. In the world of magic, a spellbook is often referred to as a grimoire or book of shadows. Because these books contain powerful spells, they are usually kept secret. In legend and lore, they are sometimes protected with enchantments that prevent them being opened by the wrong person. In some cases, they only open for the owner. In other instances, the binding is locked, and the lock itself is magical.

Book of Shadows on TV

The witches of television's *Charmed* owned a Book of Shadows that had been handed down through generations of the Halliwell family. The book became the source of many plot points in the show, as evil wizards and demons were constantly trying to steal or destroy it.

Magic Circles

When casting many spells, wizards perform their rituals within a magical circle. The circle can serve to enhance the power of the spell by focusing and containing energy temporarily. Circles also protect the wizard from unwanted forces.

The Power of the Circle

In his autobiography, the Renaissance author Benvenuto Cellini describes an incident in which he met a wizard from Sicily. The wizard took Cellini and several other men to the Colosseum in Rome at night and, having drawn a magical circle around them, conjured a group of demons to whom Cellini put several questions. However, as the number of demons increased, several of those within the circle began to be very frightened. After a time, the demons began to disperse; none had come within the boundaries of the magic circle created by the wizard.

One theory suggests that the power of a magical circle comes from the fact that it matches the path of the planets around the sun. Thus, as scholars have remarked, the lower regions mirror the upper heavens. The wizard wrote or spoke the names of entities that inhabited these upper spheres, showing them that he had created a replica of their world that they could enter and converse with him. This, at any rate, was the view during the Middle Ages. However, circles were used in magic rituals long before humankind realized the planets revolved around the sun, and today we know that the path planets follow around the sun is, in fact, elliptical.

Herbs and Roots

Wizards are very much in touch with the natural world and know what substances possess magical properties. They are particularly knowledgeable in the magic of herbs and roots; these can be dried and pounded into a powder, mixed in a magical potion, or burned to produce various magical effects. On occasion, burning herbs can cause changes in the mind of the wizard and/or his subjects, giving them visions that can later be interpreted. Many plants also contain healing properties.

SPELLCASTING

When the wizard has assembled his materials, drawn his pentagram or circle, readied his cauldron, and has his wand firmly in hand, it's time to cast a spell. The ease or difficulty of spells varies, and wizards with different levels of experience can cast more or less complex enchantments. As mentioned in the previous chapter, some spells require material components, whereas others merely need a verbal component—that is, an incantation.

It is, however, of great importance that the wizard be able to control the spell. This is particularly essential in the case of evocations (calling upon spirits). As an ancient fellow wizard warns H.P. Lovecraft's evil spellcaster Joseph Curwen, "I say to you againe, doe not call up Any that you can not put downe; by the Which I meane, Any that can in Turne call up somewhat against you, whereby your Powerfullest Devices may not be of use." (The archaic spelling in this case is Lovecraft's.)

When an inexperienced wizard calls upon the powers of a spirit, the results are often bad. A sixteenth-century writer, Martín del Río, tells the following story in his book *Disquisitiones Magicae*:

"There was someone who used to dine at the same table as Cornelius Agrippa [a famous magician], a very inquisitive young man. On one occasion when he was going out somewhere, Agrippa handed his wife . . . the keys of his study and gave strict instructions that no one was to enter. When a favourable moment presented itself, the rash youth started to beg the silly woman to let him go in . . . He went into the study, stumbled across *A Little Book of Invocations*, and read it [aloud]. Well now, he was disturbed by a knocking at the door but continued to read. The unknown person knocked again and, as the young man, (who had no experience in these matters), made no reply, a demon entered. 'Why have I been summoned?' he asked. 'What am I being told to do?' Fear blocked the young man's voice, and the demon blocked his throat."

A wise wizard always has ready the words for laying down an apparition as well as for calling it up.

Among the most powerful words a wizard can use is the name of what he is evoking. Names are especially important in magic; to know a thing's name is to gain a measure of power over it. Many wizards are therefore reluctant to use their real names, and may have a variety of names by which they are known.

A ninth-century Jewish document, the *Toledot Yeshu*, suggests that Jesus learned the name of God and this was what gave him the power to perform his miracles. The document presents Jesus as a wizard and Judas as his main rival. Once Judas also learned God's true name, he and Jesus engaged in a magical battle, hurling spells at one another while flying through the air.

Having considered some of the major tools wizards use to work their magic, we now turn to magicians of lore and legend in all parts and at all times of the world.

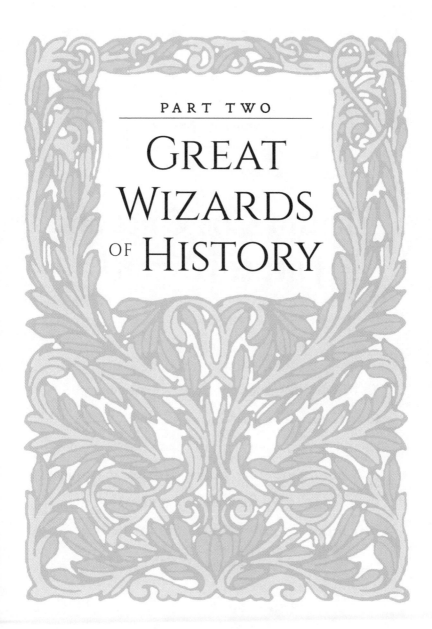

PART TWO

GREAT WIZARDS OF HISTORY

CHAPTER 4

Merlin: The Once and future Wizard

"The Merlin smiled gently. . . . 'I am dedicated to the belief that it is God's will that all men should strive for wisdom in themselves, not look to it from some other. Babes, perhaps, must have their food chewed for them by a nurse, but men may drink and eat of wisdom for themselves.' "

—MARION ZIMMER BRADLEY, *THE MISTS OF AVALON*

f all wizards, Merlin is probably the best known. By reviewing his legend, we can get a good idea of the wide range of stories about wizards and how they came into existence.

Merlin is, of course, merely part of a greater story: that of King Arthur and the Knights of the Round Table. This legend is sometimes called the Matter of Britain and has become Britain's national mythology. Certain geographic sites have become identified with it: Tintagel in Cornwall, said to be Arthur's birthplace; and Glastonbury in Somerset, which is said to be where the bodies of Arthur and his queen Guinevere were laid to rest. Glastonbury is also sometimes identified with the mysterious Isle of Avalon to which Arthur was taken after being mortally wounded by the traitor Mordred.

GEOFFREY OF MONMOUTH

The story of Merlin gets its start in a book titled *The History of the Kings of Britain*, completed by Geoffrey of Monmouth in 1136. In an age before the printing press, when all books had to be copied and decorated by hand, we can judge how popular Geoffrey's work was by the surprisingly large number of manuscripts of it that exist—more than 200.

In Geoffrey's account the evil Saxon king Vortigern tries to build a tower, but its walls keep collapsing. He learns from his court magicians that the walls will not stand unless the foundations are sprinkled with the blood of a fatherless boy. His troops find such a boy, Merlin, and bring him before the king. Merlin, however, shows the king that beneath the walls' foundations are two fighting dragons that are the cause of the tower's instability. Merlin uses the occasion to prophesy the eventual triumph of the native Britons over the Saxon invaders.

Shortly after, the Roman soldier Ambrosius Aurelianus and his brother Uther cross the Channel and defeat Vortigern in battle. Merlin joins Ambrosius's court and proves himself useful. When Ambrosius wishes to honor a group of men slain by the Saxons, Merlin advises him that only a group of giant standing stones in Ireland will be a fit memorial. Using powerful magic, he brings the stones from Ireland and reassembles them, creating the monument that we call Stonehenge.

When Ambrosius dies, Uther succeeds him. After this we have the familiar story of Uther falling in love with Ygrain, wife of the Duke of Cornwall. By the king's appeal, Merlin changes Uther into the likeness of the duke and Ygrain sleeps with him under the impression that she is sleeping with her husband. In this way, Arthur is conceived.

At this point in Geoffrey's story, Merlin disappears. There is none of the business of the sword in the stone or Merlin's later connection to the reign of Arthur. However, book seven of Geoffrey's work was entirely devoted to Merlin's prophecies, and this chapter had its own life, firmly establishing Merlin's reputation as a prophet.

Geoffrey's work was translated into Anglo-Norman by Wace and from that version to Middle English by Layamon. From the latter we get one more scene of Merlin returning to court to advise Uther, but still nothing about the sword in the stone.

ROBERT DE BORON

Robert de Boron's *Merlin*, written in about 1200, tells the story, alluded to earlier, of Merlin's diabolical parentage. In this, Merlin's prophetic abilities are conceived of as a gift from God, a result of his mother's faithful adherence to Christianity. In addition to moving the Giant's Dance (Stonehenge) from Ireland to England, de Boron's Merlin established the Round Table at Carlisle (although contrary to later legend, he does so during Uther's reign, not Arthur's).

Now, at last, we get the story of the sword lodged in the stone as a means of proving Arthur's true paternity and his right to sit on the throne. De Boron presents Merlin as the prime mover in these events.

Angel or Devil?

Some have compared Merlin's role in Arthur's enthroning to Faust's demonic advisor, Mephistopheles. It's certainly true that Merlin has no moral compunction about enabling Uther in what amounts to a rape of Ygrain. However, he could argue that what he did, he did for the greater good of Britain under Arthur's rule.

Following Arthur's elevation to the throne, Merlin supplies him with the sword Excalibur and prophecies about the end of Arthur and his knights. He also foretells such events as the quest for the Holy Grail, the love affair between Tristan and Isolde, and his own death. This comes at the hands of an unscrupulous young woman named Nyneve, who seduces the aging enchanter, steals his secrets from him, and finally imprisons him in a cave, blocking the entrance with a great rock.

THOMAS MALORY

Close to 300 years later, much the same story was told by a disreputable English knight, Sir Thomas Malory, in his *Le Morte d'Arthur*. One reason for its popularity (apart from the fact that in the fifteenth century people loved hearing tales of the legendary king) is that it was among the first books in England produced by a new technology: the printing press.

The fall of Arthur

The great fantasist J.R.R. Tolkien at one time contemplated writing an alliterative poem (that is, a poem in which the first half of each line contained a sound also found in the second half of the line) about the death of Arthur and went so far as to compose nearly 1,000 lines. The poem remained unpublished until the author's son, Christopher Tolkien, arranged for its publication in an annotated edition in 2013.

Malory's Merlin is similar to de Boron's, but Merlin's prophetic side is somewhat less emphasized. Malory also changed Nyneve's name to Nimue. Malory used as his main source a five-part French romance known as *The Vulgate Cycle*, as well as two English poems called by modern scholars *The Alliterative Morte Arthure* and *The Stanzaic Morte Arthur*.

THE LADY OF THE LAKE
TELLETH ARTHVR OF THE
SWORD EXCALIBVR

LATER AUTHORS

Although with Malory, the story of Merlin as we're familiar with it was complete, other authors continued to tell the tale of the great magician with significant variations. In the nineteenth century, the poet Alfred, Lord Tennyson produced a great cycle of Arthurian poems, *Idylls of the King*. These included the poem "Merlin and Vivien," which tells the story of Merlin's downfall. Tennyson adopts the medieval tradition in which Malory's Nimue becomes Vivien, the Lady of the Lake, who grants Arthur Excalibur. In the poem, Vivien plays a far more destructive role than in previous versions of the story. Having attached herself to Guinevere's entourage, she sows rumors in the court about the affair between Sir Lancelot and the queen. Having tried and failed to seduce Arthur, she turns to Merlin.

> "And after that, she set herself to gain
> Him, the most famous man of all those times,
> Merlin, who knew the range of all their arts,
> Had built the King his havens, ships, and halls,
> Was also Bard, and knew the starry heavens;
> The people called him Wizard; whom at first
> She played about with slight and sprightly talk,
> And vivid smiles, and faintly-venomed points
> Of slander, glancing here and grazing there;
> And yielding to his kindlier moods, the Seer
> Would watch her at her petulance, and play,
> Even when they seemed unloveable, and laugh
> As those that watch a kitten; thus he grew
> Tolerant of what he half disdained, and she,
> Perceiving that she was but half disdained,

> Began to break her sports with graver fits,
> Turn red or pale, would often when they met
> Sigh fully, or all-silent gaze upon him
> With such a fixt devotion, that the old man,
> Though doubtful, felt the flattery, and at times
> Would flatter his own wish in age for love . . ."

Playing on the elderly wizard's weakness, his "wish in age for love," Vivien worms his magical secrets from him and finally casts a spell that imprisons him in an oak tree.

Several later authors and storytellers have rung the changes on this version. Mary Stewart, in *The Last Enchantment*, has Merlin and Niniane (as she's called) fall genuinely and deeply in love. Their romantic idyll, though, is broken by Merlin's sudden illness and apparent death. Mourning him, Niniane arranges for him to be buried in his beloved crystal cave. When he finally awakens much later, he has to struggle hard to escape from his tomb and send word to Camelot that he's very much alive. Niniane, however, has moved on to another love and is established as the new court wizard. Merlin accepts her new relationship and returns to his cave to live out his days as a hermit.

In John Boorman's film *Excalibur*, it is Morgan le Fay who attempts to imprison Merlin in a crystal-filled cavern. She uses her wiles to wheedle from him the Charm of Making, and with it she imprisons him. However, the mortal blow to him is struck when Lancelot's treachery to Arthur is revealed and the kingdom, divided against itself, begins a long decline into chaos. Thereafter, Merlin can only return to the mortal world as a dream.

The Power in a Name

Over the centuries, Merlin's name has become a byword for mystery and intrigue. In his bestselling spy novel *Tinker, Tailor, Soldier, Spy*, John Le Carré makes good use of it. The Circus (the British spy agency in Le Carre's novels) has acquired a top-secret Kremlin source with unparalleled access to the highest levels of policy making in the Soviet government. The source code name? Merlin. His product is code-named Witchcraft.

Le Carre spins an exciting tale of double-dealing and plots within plots within plots. In the end, Merlin is revealed to be not all he appears.

MARK TWAIN AND MERLIN

One of the most amusing—and devastating—portraits of Merlin comes at the hands of America's premier nineteenth-century satirist. In 1889, Mark Twain published *A Connecticut Yankee in King Arthur's Court*. The novel tells the story of a man from the nineteenth century who finds himself magically transported to Camelot. There, filled with the scientific and technical knowledge of his age, he confronts a people who are bound in superstition and ignorance. To the Yankee (whose name is Hank Morgan, but is usually known in Camelot by his title, The Boss), Merlin embodies everything that is wrong with the time. Merlin is a pretend magician—that is, he fools the court of Arthur through cheap tricks and is powerless beside the very real science that The Boss commands. When someone brings news to the Yankee that Merlin is trying to injure him with a spell, his contempt bursts into the open:

> "Merlin has wrought a spell! *Merlin*, forsooth! That cheap old humbug, that maundering old ass? Bosh, pure bosh, the silliest bosh in the world! Why, it does seem to me that of all the childish, idiotic, chuckle-headed, chicken-livered superstitions that ev—oh, damn Merlin!"

In an effort to break Merlin's hold over Arthur, The Boss, once he has established himself as an advisor to the king, takes an opportunity to blow up Merlin's tower, apparently with magic (in reality, with gunpowder). To further undermine the magician's reputation, he orders that Merlin should spend his time predicting the weather.

> "He was the worst weather failure in the kingdom. Whenever he ordered up the danger-signals along the coast there was a week's dead calm, sure, and every time he prophesied fair weather it rained brickbats."

In the end, tragically, it is Merlin who triumphs. Following Arthur's death at the hands of the treacherous Mordred, The Boss and his fifty-two supporters have fought a battle against the massed chivalry of

England to establish a democratic English republic. Science apparently triumphs; The Boss and his followers win, ensconcing themselves in a cave surrounded by electrified fences and guarded by machine guns. Merlin manages to make his way into the cave in disguise and casts a spell (one of his few that work) on The Boss that puts the Yankee to sleep for thirteen centuries. He will wake up back in his own time. As for Merlin, "Then such a delirium of silly laughter overtook him that he reeled about like a drunken man, and presently fetched up against one of our wires. His mouth is spread open yet; apparently he is still laughing. I suppose the face will retain that petrified laugh until the corpse turns to dust."

 ## MERLIN IN FILM AND TELEVISION

Filmmakers find Merlin irresistible because he fits so well the traditional idea of a wizard. Here are a few of the movies in which the character appears and the actors who played him:

- *The Sorcerer's Apprentice* (2010) James A. Stephens
- *Merlin: The Return* (2000) Rik Mayall
- *A Kid in King Arthur's Court* (1995) Ron Moody
- *Excalibur* (1981) Nicol Williamson
- *The Spaceman and King Arthur* (1979) Ron Moody
- *Son of Dracula* (1974) Ringo Starr

Williamson's portrayal in *Excalibur* is probably the one that tries to stay as true to its source material as possible. Merlin is mysterious, appearing when least expected. Yet he is also vulnerable to error or to lack of foresight.

When young Arthur is battling to establish his birthright to the throne, he is challenged by Sir Uryens, who shouts angrily, "You're not even a knight."

"You are right," agrees Arthur. "I am not yet a knight. You, Uryens, will knight me." With these words, he hands Excalibur to his opponent and kneels before him.

"What's this?" exclaims Merlin. "I never saw this!"

All turns out well. Uryens, overcome by the power of the sword and by the strength that shines from Arthur, knights him and swears allegiance to him as king. But we see that Merlin can, on occasion, be as blind to the future as any mortal.

Monty Python and Tim

One of the best-known—and goofiest—film versions of the Arthurian legend is the one made by the troupe of comedians calling themselves Monty Python. When the Pythons (Eric Idle, John Cleese, Michael Palin, Terry Jones, Graham Chapman, and Terry Gilliam) released *Monty Python and the Holy Grail* in 1975 they had evidently decided to make due without the character of Merlin. However, this being Arthur's England (complete with the Holy Hand Grenade of Antioch, a Black Knight, who continues to fight bravely even after his arms and legs are chopped off, and a giant wooden rabbit), a different enchanter does put in an appearance. While traversing a bleak stretch of rocky mountainside in search of a mystical cave, Arthur and his knights encounter a raggedly clad wizard, hurling fire bolts at distant rocks.

"There are some," he coldly informs them, "some who call me . . . *Tim!*"

The Sword in the Stone

In 1963, Disney released an animated film version of T.H. White's classic story of young King Arthur. Apart from Sebastian Cabot (later to become famous as Mr. French on television's *Family Affair*), the voices cast were unknown actors. The film portrays Merlin, much as White had depicted him, as a mildly eccentric, absent-minded old gentleman who happens to be a wizard. However, the moviemakers removed several large elements from the story (for example, in the book young Wart, to further his education, is taken by Merlin to watch some real knights fighting) and threw in by way of compensation a magical duel between Merlin and Madam Mim, an unscrupulous fellow sorcerer. The duel had appeared in White's original version of the story published in 1938, but was removed by him for the 1958 revision.

A wizards' duel, as Wart discovers while he and Merlin's owl, Archimedes, watch from a safe distance, consists of the two magicians changing themselves into animals and trying in these different forms to destroy each other. Madam Mim, to no one's surprise, cheats, turning herself invisible, something explicitly prohibited by the rules. She then changes in quick succession into an alligator, a fox, a hen, an elephant, a tiger, a rattlesnake, and a rhinoceros. Finally, she transforms into a fire-breathing dragon.

Merlin: Now, now, Mim, Mim, no . . . no dragons, remember?
Madame Mim: Did I say no purple dragons? Did I?

Merlin promptly disappears and Mim accuses him of cheating.

"Madam," the elderly wizard answers in a dignified manner, "I have not disappeared. I'm very tiny. I am a germ. A rare disease. I am called malignalitaloptereosis . . . and you caught me, Mim!"

The sequence ends with Mim in bed in her cottage, looking pale and sickly as Merlin and Wart bid her farewell.

King Arthur

One distinctly odd take on the legend of Merlin comes from the 2004 film *King Arthur*, starring Keira Knightley and Clive Owen as Guinevere and Arthur. This film is an attempt to place the Arthurian legend in the context of late Roman Britain and to largely strip it of its magical elements. Arthur is a Roman cavalry officer, stationed in Britain and attempting to keep order against the marauding Woads, led by the mysterious figure of Merlin. At the same time, Britain is repeatedly subjected to attacks by the Saxons, a Germanic people.

Guinevere is a Woad, captured by Arthur. She reveals to him that her father is Merlin and eventually arranges a meeting between the two men. Arthur, it turns out, is part Woad on his mother's side, and Merlin wants to arrange an alliance between the Woads and the Romans to fight off the Saxons.

"This is beyond understanding," said the king. "You are the wisest man alive. You know what is preparing. Why do you not make a plan to save yourself?"

And Merlin said quietly, "Because I am wise. In the combat between wisdom and feeling, wisdom never wins."

—JOHN STEINBECK, *THE ACTS OF KING ARTHUR AND HIS NOBLE KNIGHTS*

In the climactic battle, Arthur and the Woads defeat the Saxons, but at the cost of Lancelot, Arthur's friend. Arthur and Guinevere become the leaders of the resistance to the Saxon invasion, and Merlin proclaims Arthur king of Britain.

MERLIN ON THE SMALL SCREEN

The famous wizard is no stranger to television. He has appeared in several made-for-TV adaptations of Twain's *A Connecticut Yankee* as well as in two mini-series, *Merlin* (1998), starring Sam Neill and Miranda Richardson, and *Merlin's Apprentice* (2006), plus a BBC-produced series *Merlin*, which ran from 2008 to 2012. Reaching back further, beginning in 1981, *Mr. Merlin*, starring Barnard Hughes as the magician, ran two seasons.

TV's *Merlin*

Of all the portrayals of the magician on television, Sam Neill's is probably the best known. In this version we get a new explanation of the enchanter's parentage: He is magically implanted in his mother by Mab (Miranda Richardson), the fairy queen, and raised by a woman who refuses to give him up to Mab, because the fairy wants to use Merlin as a weapon to turn people against Christianity and back to the Old Ways.

The Coming of the New God

The idea that Merlin represents pre-Christian religion in Britain and, as such, struggles against the "One God" is widespread in modern versions of the story. It pops up, for example, in *Excalibur* and in Mary Stewart's *The Crystal Cave* and Marion Zimmer Bradley's *The Mists of Avalon*. However, it has no foundation in the older tradition of Merlin stories. Thomas Malory's *Le Morte d'Arthur*, for example, takes place in a thoroughly Christian context.

Queen Mab is thus set up as Merlin's main antagonist, necessitating Merlin's involvement in the conception and raising of Arthur, whom the wizard sees as his main weapon against Mab. Merlin also meets Nimue when they're about the same age, another departure from tradition.

The series won a number of awards, and Neill's performance as Merlin was widely hailed by critics. He returned to the role in *Merlin's Apprentice*.

The BBC's *Merlin*

Strongly influenced by the success of American television's *Smallville* (the story of Superman's early years), the BBC launched *Merlin* in 2008, starring Colin Morgan as Merlin and Bradley James as Arthur. The story takes place entirely during the youth of both characters and establishes their relationship as one of friendship within a master-servant context.

In this version of the story, there is no suggestion of Arthur being secretly raised apart from the royal court. He is Uther's son (Uther is played by Anthony Head, familiar to fans of *Buffy the Vampire Slayer* as Giles) and is very much aware that he is the prince and heir apparent to the throne. Merlin becomes his servant, but deliberately conceals his magical abilities from Arthur and pretty much everyone else. This is necessary because Uther has launched a campaign against magic, outlawing its use on pain of death. As previously mentioned, Merlin befriends a dragon (voiced by John Hurt) who gives him advice from time to time. The dragon explains that Merlin must, at all costs, protect Arthur from danger, so Merlin has to constantly struggle to hide his magic while at the same time using it to defeat various enemies of the prince. Moreover, he must deal with Arthur's arrogance and counter it with his own wit.

Arthur: I warn you, I've been trained to kill since birth.
Merlin: Wow. And how long have you been training to be a prat?
Arthur: You can't address me like that.
Merlin: Sorry. How long have you been training to be a prat, my lord?"

Fortunately, Arthur has enough self-awareness to usually notice when he's behaving like a self-centered ass. In a sense, the series is very much about two young men growing up together and forming a bond of friendship that will serve them well for the rest of their lives.

Morgan le Fay is named Morgana in the series and is initially friends with both Arthur and Merlin. However, she turns against them when Uther's betrayals of her parents become clear. Guinevere is far from a princess; in fact, she's one of the common folk and first befriends Merlin, then Arthur, and then falls in love with and marries the prince (against Uther's objections).

The series was extremely popular in Britain and was exported to American television beginning in 2009.

A WIZARD FOR THE AGES

In legend, Merlin embodies everything a wizard should be. This perhaps explains the hundreds, if not thousands, of variants on his story that have been created over the centuries. As he says to the evil witch Morgause in Mary Stewart's novel *The Hollow Hills*:

> "I am nothing, yes; I am air and darkness, a word, a promise. I watch in the crystal and I wait in the hollow hills. But out there in the light I have a young king and a bright sword to do my work for me, and build what will stand when my name is only a word for forgotten songs and outworn wisdom, and when your name, Morgause, is only a hissing in the dark."

Now we turn to the other wizards who inhabit the world and bring to it their own far-reaching magic.

CHAPTER 5

Wizards of the West

"But I'll tell you something: I think you're magicians because you're unhappy. A magician is strong because he feels pain. He feels the difference between what the world is and what he would make of it. Or what did you think that stuff in your chest was? A magician is strong because he hurts more than others. His wound is his strength."

—Dean Fogg, *The Magicians* by Lev Grossman

elief in magic can be traced back to the very earliest stages of human existence, but in the West we find it first systematized in ancient Greece and in the Persian Empire. The Persian term *mageia*, from which we get the word "magic," refers to rituals and ceremonies practiced by a *magos* (plural, *magoi*). Herodotus, one of the earliest of Greek chroniclers, says that *magoi* presided over funerals and other sacred rituals. They could also control the weather. When the Persian fleet was being pounded by a great storm and was in danger of being destroyed, the Persian *magoi* worked their spells and managed to quiet the raging winds.

Despite this, there seems to have been a disreputable air about magic and wizards in the ancient world. In the play *Oedipus the King* by Sophocles, the seer Tiresias is a relatively unsympathetic character. Herodotus, in his *Histories* makes similar disdainful comments about *magoi*, even when they perform useful services.

The rise of the Roman Empire from the second century B.C. on meant that magical practices from around the Mediterranean flowed into Europe. The earliest Roman law code, the Twelve Tablets, makes mention of bad magical practices that are outlawed, so evidently this was enough of a problem to draw attention to it. Rome became an attractant to magical rituals and to wizards from Greece, Egypt, Persia, and ever more far-flung parts of Europe and Asia as the empire grew in strength and size.

A Magician by Edward Kelly

Casting Lots

Roman magicians had many ways of divining the future, but one of the most popular was casting lots (that is, randomly picking objects on which were inscribed various predictions). The lots were known as *sortes*, and from this Latin term came the word *sortilegium*, which eventually referred to all magical practices. Old French adopted the word and it became the root of the French *sorcellerie*. This word is, of course, the root of the English word *sorcerer*.

Roman authors sometimes mention love potions, something that wizards sold in large numbers. In the Latin epic poem *The Aeneid*, the Carthaginian queen Dido, having fallen in love with the Trojan prince Aeneas, has one of her wizards cast a love spell to ensnare him when he tells her that he must leave to found the city in Italy that is his destiny. However, the power of the gods to direct fate is greater than the spell, and Aeneas leaves Carthage and Dido. Despairing, the queen commits suicide and Aeneas, sailing away from the city, sees the smoke from her funeral pyre spread across the sky.

TABLETS AND DOLLS

Two magical objects common in the Roman period that extended into the Middle Ages were the curse tablet and the magical doll.

Curse tablets were objects, often wooden or stone slabs, on which a wizard would inscribe a curse or incantation, usually aimed at a particular person. Once he completed the incantation, he would bury the tablet, often in a place believed to have magical power, such as a graveyard. Archaeologists have found many samples of such tablets.

" 'Enemies,' the wizard said, 'are the price of honour.' "

—TERRY GOODKIND,
DEBT OF BONES

The dolls were used in much the way we think of voodoo dolls. The wizard would make a representation of the person to be afflicted, speak spells over it, and then either bury or burn it. It's notable that this practice eventually made its way across the Atlantic to the New World. In the Salem witch trials of 1692, several of the accused witches were charged with making dolls, or "poppets" as they are now called, as a means of attacking members of the community.

HERMES TRISMEGISTUS

Egypt supplied Rome with a rich magical tradition. At some point during the second and third centuries A.D., a large body of Egyptian magical literature was translated into Latin and rapidly spread among wizards of the empire. These writings, which were probably produced originally at very different times and places, were attributed to Hermes Trismegistus, a mythical wizard who seems to have had aspects of the Egyptian god Thoth as well as the Greek god Hermes. The material included astrological and alchemical information as well as various mystical rites and beliefs.

After the collapse of the Roman Empire in the fourth century, much of this material was lost or forgotten. During the Middle Ages, the main source of manuscript copying was the Catholic Church, and monks were little inclined to copy manuscripts that seemed well outside the Christian tradition. However, beginning in the fourteenth century and on into the Renaissance, the Corpus Hermeticum was rediscovered in Western Europe.

Pagan Prophet

Although Hermes Trismegistus has his roots in pagan society, many later Christian writers, including St. Thomas Aquinas, St. Augustine, and Ralph Waldo Emerson, believed that his writings (or, at any rate, the writings attributed to him) were prophetic of the coming of Christianity.

Hermeticism

The Corpus Hermeticum became the basis for Hermeticism, an esoteric tradition in Western religious thought. This tradition is founded on the idea that there is a secret body of wisdom with a distinctly magical character that has been largely hidden from society, but nonetheless has been passed down from generation to generation.

The writings attributed to Hermes Trismegistus emerged into Europe at a significant point when science was beginning to divorce itself from its magical roots. In the seventeenth century, the beginning of an age of scientific revolution, figures such as Isaac Newton studied the Corpus Hermeticum and absorbed what they could from it.

Essentially, Hermeticism argues that there are three kinds of magic:

I. Astrology. We've already discussed the idea that wizards interpret the movement of the heavenly bodies and their influence on our lives. Hermes detailed this practice and emphasized its importance.

2. Alchemy. As previously mentioned, this is the study of chemicals and the attempt to turn base metals into gold, either physically or symbolically. Hermes, in his writings, connected it to the study of the spiritual foundations of matter and how it relates to life and death.

3. Theurgy. This is the divinely inspired magical energy that Hermes believed came directly from the gods. It is opposed to evil magic, Goetia, which draws its power from demons.

All these concepts were studied eagerly by Renaissance thinkers. Some tried to combine them with other mystical traditions, such as the

Pieter Bruegel the Elder - The Alchemist (1558, Ink on paper) Engraved by Philips Galle

Jewish Kabbalah. Hermetic thought faded somewhat during the seventeenth and eighteenth centuries but had a rebirth in the nineteenth century, when it was studied by many prominent people and became part of the foundation of such mystical groups as the Order of the Golden Dawn, the Rosicrucians, and the Theosophical Society.

In all this development, there remains the central figure of Hermes Trismegistus, half mortal wizard and half god. The Corpus Hermeticum is an important element of the wizarding tradition in Western Europe.

WIZARDS IN THE EARLY MIDDLE AGES

The single biggest threat to wizards in Western Europe began in 312 A.D. when Constantine was victorious at the Battle of the Milvian Bridge outside Rome. Constantine, one of the contenders for the title of Roman emperor, won the battle, he believed, because he had seen the sign of the cross in the sky before the fighting began. As a result, Constantine began the process of converting to Christianity and embarked on a political and cultural path that would, within a hundred years, spread the hitherto small and obscure Christian religion throughout the empire.

Christians believed that miracles came from God. Magic, such as that practiced by wizards, on the other hand, they thought was inspired by the devil and must be not only repudiated but wiped out.

Apollonius of Tyana

Even before Constantine's victory, wizards in the West were under a good deal of suspicion by political forces. We have an interesting illustration of this in Apollonius of Tyana, a contemporary of Jesus, whose story was told by the author Philostratus.

Apollonius began by studying Greek philosophers. Having exhausted their wisdom, he did
what many wizards chose to do and traveled
to the East. He visited Egypt, Persia, and
India, centers of magical learning, where he
absorbed the techniques of yogic levitation
and found an abundance of secret wisdom
(it's even possible, of course, that he familiar-
ized himself with the Corpus Hermeticum).

Apollonius and Islam

Through Philostratus's biography, Apollonius's fame spread, and after the
rise of Islam in the eighth and ninth centuries, he became a well-known
figure in the eastern Mediterranean world as well as the West. Islamic writers, who named him Balinas or Ablus, considered him to be a master of
alchemy and astrology and attributed several books to him. These include:

- *Book of the Secret of Creation*
- *Treatise on the Influence of the Spiritual Beings on the Composite
  Things*
- *The Great Book of Talismans*
- *Book of the Sage Ablus*

Having returned to Greece, he gained a reputation as a soothsayer.
He continued his travels to ancient Troy, where he spoke with the ghost of
the mighty Achilles. In due time, these activities and others brought him
to the attention of the authorities, who were worried that he was drawing
his powers from evil spirits and who arrested him. It's not clear how his
trial ended, but Apollonius seems to have had no hesitation in defending
himself, even in front of the emperor.

Simon Magus

By the fourth century, when the Emperor Constantine legalized Christianity, there had already grown up a tradition of conflict between wizards and the Christian faithful. The most famous example involves Simon of Samaria, also known as Simon Magus (that is, Simon the Magician).

After Jesus's death, his disciples fanned out and began to spread the word that Jesus was the Christ, savior of mankind. Simon, so the story goes, was sufficiently impressed by St. Peter's preaching that he con-verted to Christianity. How-ever, he also offered to make Peter a present of his magi-cal learning. He would, he said, teach Peter how to do magic—but only for a price. Peter indignantly refused the offer, and Simon's name became attached in the Middle Ages to the sin of simony, the buying and sell-ing of church office.

The story of Simon and Peter appears in the Acts of the Apostles. However, the unauthorized Apocry-phal work *The Acts of Peter* contains other accounts. In one, for example, Simon by his magic was able to make

The death of Simon Magus

a dead man twitch; however, Peter, calling upon the power of God, brought the man to life. Simon used his powers to levitate himself, but Peter brought him back to earth. In each case, divine power was shown to be superior to a wizard's worldly magic.

The whole concept of wizards and magic presented a worrying situation for early Christians. After all, the infant Jesus had been visited by three magi from the East. When he was older, he worked miracles that looked very much like magic. In fact, there was a heretical belief that Jesus, at some time in his youth, had visited Egypt and learned his skills from Egyptian wizards. It has also been suggested that he traveled to India and learned from the wise men there.

For this reason Christians carefully distinguished between the kind of magic displayed by Simon Magus and the divine miracles Jesus used to ensure the faith of his followers. Simon's powers, they claimed, were of diabolical origins, whereas Jesus was able to perform his miracles because he was the Son of God. As well, wherever they came to power Christians were vigorous in prosecuting accused witches and wizards.

Wizards and Witches

The accusation of wizardry or witchcraft became a handy tool for the medieval church in its battle against heretics and political enemies. When Joan of Arc was captured by the English during the Hundred Years War, she was accused of witchcraft, among other things. The church also hurled the charge of wizardry against Muhammad and his followers in the religion of Islam.

WIZARDS IN THE HIGH MIDDLE AGES

Around the twelfth century, Europe seemed to stretch and shake itself, shrugging off the intellectual and economic stagnation of the previous 500 years. Between 1100 and 1250, the great universities were founded in Paris, Bologna, Oxford, Cambridge, Padua, and elsewhere. This meant that there was now a body of professional learned men, scholars, who studied alchemy, astrology, and other aspects of magic. It also meant there was interest in writing down spells, particularly those that were commonly employed, such as healing spells.

As populations grew, especially in the cities, people needed increased supplies of food. This meant that wizards sought spells to increase the fertility of crops and fight off agricultural blights.

Relics

One magical item that assumed great importance during the High Middle Ages (1001–1300) was the relic, an object that has a strong association with a holy person and for that reason has acquired magical powers. Often, medieval relics were the bones, hair, or bits of clothing that had once belonged to saints. As communications expanded across the continent, a brisk trade in these powerful items arose. That trade was enhanced by the Crusades—a series of expeditions by Christian knights to the Holy Land, aiming to wrest Jerusalem from the Muslims and restore it to Christian rule. These knights actively sought out relics and brought them back by the trunkload.

Relics of fabled heroes in the Classical period (fourth and fifth centuries B.C.) had been venerated, too, but rarely possessed any special magical power. The head of Orpheus the bard, though, is said to have been taken to the island of Lesbos, where it served as an oracle, though people didn't expect it to heal their injuries.

All this changed in the Middle Ages. Relics of Christian saints were highly prized, not only for their religious significance but because they could work magic. Medieval literature is full of accounts of people who were sick or dying, but were touched by relics and experienced miraculous recoveries.

An Appropriate Relic Setting

In addition to their spiritual/magical value, relics possessed real monetary value, and people who owned them often created elaborate reliquaries to hold them. The more important the relic, the more magnificent and costly the reliquary in which it was housed.

Relics were the objects of rivalry, theft, and minor wars. Cathedrals competed with one another for the biggest and most impressive relics. Naturally, the best relics and the ones believed to have the most magical power were those directly associated with Christ. Pilgrims traveling in Europe in the thirteenth century could have found dozens of shards of the "True Cross" (also called the Holy Rood), the cross on which Jesus was crucified. They could also have marveled at pieces of the crown of thorns, bits of the manger in Bethlehem where the Christ child was born, and the tip of the spear with which a Roman soldier pierced Jesus's side as he was dying on the cross.

In the fourteenth century, the English writer Geoffrey Chaucer composed a series of stories supposedly told by pilgrims on their way to Canterbury Cathedral to pay homage to the shrine of St. Thomas Becket, among the most famous English saints. The pilgrimage, Chaucer makes clear, is to take advantage of the magical healing power of the saint's relics ("he who had helped them when they were sick"). The stories were titled *The Canterbury Tales* and became one of the most famous works of English literature ever written.

Wizard Relics

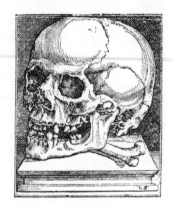

Most of the relics in the Middle Ages were Christian in nature, although the tradition they drew on was closely allied with wizardly magic. Wizards also possessed relics and used them in spells.

Among the most common of such relics was the human skull. Wizards are often depicted in their laboratories with skulls or human skeletons. During the late Middle Ages and early Renaissance, the science of anatomy advanced considerably, partly due to the influx of medical texts into Western Europe from the Middle East. As a result, doctors became much more aware of the importance of the skull and the brain in human functioning.

Relics in Modern Wizardry

Magical relics continue to play an important role in tales of modern wizards. For instance, Harry Potter's wand contains a tail feather of a phoenix, a magical bird that bursts into flame when it dies and is reborn from the ashes. Harry Dresden's wizarding equipment includes, among other things, a talking skull named Bob who is able to advise him from time to time about magical problems.

WIZARDS IN THE RENAISSANCE

A great revival of art, learning, and culture began in the fifteenth century and continued until the late sixteenth century. Building on the foundations of the late Middle Ages, it created a culture that was, among other things, fascinated with all things magical. The period saw, for example, an increased production of wizard spellbooks (also known as grimoires). Two in particular were of importance: the *Clavicula Salomonis* or *Key of Solomon*, written sometime in the fourteenth or fifteenth century, and the *Lemegeton*, also known as the *Lesser Key of Solomon*, compiled in the late sixteenth century.

The *Clavicula Salomonis*

The *Key of Solomon*'s author is unknown, although as the title makes clear, there was an attempt to attribute it to King Solomon, whom tradition held to have been a mighty wizard. The enchanter must take a ritual bath and engage in prayer. This is followed by three days of fasting and praying before the spell is actually cast.

The magician creates a magic circle and intones appropriate prayers to various spirits and angels. Some of the spells call for material components. If

The Magic Circle by John William Waterhouse
(1849–1917)

the spell has been properly cast, spirits will appear to the wizard whom he can control and direct. Finally, when he is finished he must dismiss them.

Conjuring Spirits

The *Key of Solomon* gives the full text of the invocation that is to be used when conjuring spirits. It begins:

"O ye Spirits, ye I conjure by the Power, Wisdom, and Virtue of the Spirit of God, by the uncreate Divine Knowledge, by the vast Mercy of God, by the Strength of God, by the Greatness of God, by the Unity of God; and by the Holy Name of God EHEIEH, which is the root, trunk, source, and origin of all the other Divine Names, whence they all draw their life and their virtue, which Adam having invoked, he acquired the knowledge of all created things."

Other chapters of the work give detailed instructions on drawing pentagrams and creating other magical equipment.

The *Lemegeton*

This work is divided into five parts. The first part, called the *Goetia*, deals with dark magic and shows wizards how to summon demons and other dark beings, and also includes explanations for how the wizard can take himself to other realms and commune with such spirits in their own territory. The book lists seventy-two spirits, a number associated with the Kabbalah's seventy-two names of God. The second part gives a list of good and bad spirits, their status and their attributes, along with how to conjure them. The spirits can do a great deal, ranging from making people fall in love to creating music out of thin air.

The third part, called the *Ars Paulina*, describes the twenty-four angels of the hours of the day and night, plus those of the seven planets known at the time.

An Incense for Wizards

The *Lemegeton* gives a recipe for an incense that can be used by wizards in scrying—that is, looking into crystal balls or other objects to see beyond the scope of ordinary human vision. The incense is composed of pepperwort, nutmeg, lignum ales, saffron, cinnamon, myrtle, and mastic. These spices were connected with the seven planets that were known at the time.

The fourth, *Ars Almadel*, discusses the chief angels of the four directions or corners of the world, their powers and attributes, and how to work with these beings. It also instructs the reader in how to create a magic tabletop using wax inscribed with various designs and symbols. The fifth part contains the prayers and incantations used by Solomon, said to have been revealed by the angel Michael.

John Dee

Of all Renaissance magic users, John Dee was unquestionably the most famous in his time. His position at Queen Elizabeth's court helped to ensure his high reputation as well as protect him from attacks by the church.

He was born in 1527 and attended Trinity College in Cambridge the year after it was established by Henry VIII. There he showed a great aptitude for mathematics as well as for the more practical aspects of engineering.

The Flying Dung Beetle

During his time at Cambridge, Dee staged a production of *Peace*, a play by the ancient Greek author Aristophanes. In the play, the hero tries to reach Zeus's palace in the skies, attempting the journey on several devices and finally settling for a flying creature. Dee built a large dung beetle and, through an ingenious series of pulleys and wires, actually got it to apparently lift off the ground and seemingly "fly" through the hall. Though he showed afterward how the effect was achieved, some murmured that he must have received the aid of dark magic. This was the beginning of Dee's reputation as a wizard.

FAUST

Of all Elizabethan literary wizards, none, perhaps, was as well known as Faust. This is due in large measure to the play *Dr. Faustus* by Shakespeare's contemporary Christopher Marlowe (1564–1593).

It's very possible, in fact probable, that Marlowe and others who wrote about Faust based their stories on a real person. As early as 1507, there is mention in a letter of someone named George Sabellicus, "Faust the Young." According to the letter writer, Abbot Johannes Trithemius, Faust was going from city to city in the German kingdoms suggesting he was "the fount from which necromancers flow, an astrologer, a second magus." The first magus, scholars assume, was Simon Magus (mentioned earlier in this chapter). Faust claimed that he could bring the dead back to life, that he had wide-ranging knowledge of ancient philosophers, as well as an extensive knowledge of alchemy. References to him continue over the next few decades, although this was a time of tremendous upheaval in the German-speaking world, since 1517 when Martin Luther began the Protestant Reformation in Wittenberg. Luther evidently was aware of

Faust and referred to him once or twice as inspired by the devil. He called Faust a *Schwartzkünstler*, that is, someone who practiced black magic.

As time passed, the stories about Faust grew more elaborate. He was said, during a lecture at the University of Erfurt, to have called up the ghosts of various historical and mythical personages, including Hector, Agamemnon, Odysseus, and the cyclops Polyphemus. In his *Chronicle*, Zacharias Hogel records that Faust confessed to him that he had sold himself to the devil. When Faust eventually died in Württemberg, there were reports of the entire house shaking. His legend was published in various forms; Marlowe got hold of one that had been translated into English and it served as the basis of his play.

In *Dr. Faustus* (the full title is *The Tragical History of Doctor Faustus*), published in 1604 after the death of its author, Faust is a character who evokes sympathy from the audience. Faust explains to the audience at the start that he has intellectually exhausted every subject that he has studied and is eager for new worlds to conquer. To resolve the question he calls upon two wizards, Valdes and Cornelius, and concludes from their advice that he should take up magic.

However, that decision comes with a clause: Faust must pledge his soul to the devil to obtain magical knowledge. Lucifer appears before him, and the two strike a bargain by the terms of which Faust will have another twenty-four years in which to master the magical arts. In this he will be aided by the infernal character Mephistopheles, who will act as his servant, as well as his liaison to the devil.

The play passes lightly over the next two and a half decades and focuses on the final scene when Mephistopheles takes Faust down to hell with him. The audience is left with the impression that Faust has regretted his bargain and would alter it if he could. Now, though, the quest for knowledge has resulted in eternal damnation. Such are the consequences of human ambition and pride.

Goethe's *Faust*

In the nineteenth century, Germany's most famous poet, Johannes Wolfgang von Goethe (1749–1832), produced a dramatic version of the Faust story that is considered by many to be among Germany's greatest works of literature. It includes some significant differences from Marlowe's version. In the first part (which bears a striking resemblance to the biblical story of Job), Mephistopheles bets God he can tempt Faust, who is God's favorite human, away from the path of righteousness. The bargain that Faust eventually makes with the demon is that Mephistopheles will serve him on earth and he will serve Mephistopheles in hell.

Faust's first act is to seduce a maiden, Margaret. The seduction ends in her death, despite Faust's efforts to save her after she is condemned to die for drowning her illegitimate child.

The second part of the play cycle is a series of scenes involving Faust's use of his magic to meet famous people, including Helen of Troy. He rises in favor with the emperor as he becomes an old man. Eventually, he is able to atone for his sins sufficiently that the bet with Mephistopheles is annulled and Faust is received into heaven.

A Faustian Pact

The adjective "Faustian" has come to mean a compromise or pact with something unpleasant for the sake of the greater good. The common theme that runs through all the versions of the Faust legend—and there are many more manifestations of it, including ballets, operas, poetry, and more—is the notion of a human who is willing to make a Satanic bargain for the sake of knowledge beyond the ken of ordinary men. In other words, magical knowledge.

The Tragedy of Magic

This is a theme of much of the literature about wizards: They attain their knowledge only through long, hard effort that often results in personal loss. "Ours, my boy, is a high and lonely destiny," says Andrew Kirke, the wizard in C.S. Lewis's *The Magician's Nephew*. That loss may be emotional, physical, or both. (For instance, Raistlin Majere, the wizard featured in the Dragonlance Chronicles, emerges from the Test of Sorcery with his health shattered and even more embittered against the world.) Tragically, that lonely destiny isolates wizards from their fellow human beings and, when combined with pride, can result in a terrifying fall. Faust exemplifies what happens when the bargain the magician makes is too great for his soul.

THE "MAGUS" VIRGIL

During the Renaissance, scholars looked for inspiration to the great works of Classical antiquity. Philosophic schools such as the Neoplatonists sprang up, dedicated to reinterpreting the works of Greek philosophers.

There was also a rediscovery of Classical literature, including *The Aeneid*, Virgil's magnificent poem about the founding of the Roman people. People of fifteenth-century Europe also discovered or created all sorts of legends about Rome's greatest poet. He was, they said, not merely a poet but also a magus.

Virgil (70–19 B.C.) was effectively the official poet to the imperial court of the first Roman emperor, Augustus Caesar. *The Aeneid* is the most important of his works; it tells the story of Aeneas, prince of Troy, ancestor of the Roman race. Virgil's popularity, considerable at the time of his death, continued throughout the Middle Ages. Some theologians argued that certain of his poems anticipated Christianity, and he came to be regarded as a prophet. From there it was an easy step to make him a magus, capable not only of foretelling the future but of performing acts of wizardry.

"They never tell you some things. They tell you mages have wonderful power and they learn all kinds of secrets. Nobody ever mentions that some secrets you don't ever want to learn."

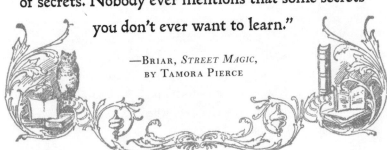

—BRIAR, *STREET MAGIC*,
BY TAMORA PIERCE

A Modern Treatment of Virgil

Noted fantasy author Avram Davidson (1923–1993) was so intrigued by the stories of Virgil the wizard that he wrote several novels about the Roman, a series he intended to call the Vergil Magus. These include:

- *The Phoenix and the Mirror*
- *Vergil in Averno*
- *The Scarlet Fig*

Four of his short stories dealing with Vergil have also been published:

- "The Other Magus," *Edges*, ed. Ursula K. Le Guin and Virginia Kidd. Pocket Books, 1980
- "Vergil and the Caged Bird," *Amazing*, January 1987
- "Vergil and the Dukos: Hic Inclusus Vitam Perdit," or "The Imitations of the King," *Asimov's*, September 1997
- "Vergil Magus: King Without Country," with Michael Swanwick, *Asimov's*, July 1998

In some stories, Virgil's father was a knight; in others the father was also a wizard. Virgil is said to have learned magic from a spirit, which he found trapped in a bottle. The spirit offered to teach Virgil magic in return for freeing it. After some bargaining, the boy agreed. The spirit imparted its various spells and incantations, and Virgil let it out of the bottle. Feeling threatened by the spirit, Virgil cleverly remarked that he didn't see how such a large being could fit into such a small bottle. The spirit dived back through the lid into the bottle's interior, and the quick-thinking boy jammed the cork back in, trapping the spirit once more.

Once, the emperor appealed to the poet to do something about the street crime in Rome. Virgil ordered everyone indoors, but only the honest people obeyed. Then the wizard brought forth a copper horse and copper rider, who trampled to death those who remained in the streets. When the thieves and murderers fought back and attempted to destroy the magical beast, Virgil added two copper dogs that tore apart those criminals who remained alive.

At last the wizard fell in love with a beautiful girl, the daughter of a sultan. He brought her away with him to Rome, but she wanted to return to her father. Virgil returned her, and after a time she agreed to go back to him. Feeling that the city of Rome was not beautiful enough for her, he created the city of Naples.

The City of Virgil

The legend of Virgil the wizard creating Naples for his lovely bride may have its foundation in the fact that the poet was educated there and lived there for a time.

THE CONTE DI CAGLIOSTRO

The Renaissance was followed by a period called the Enlightenment, which lasted for much of the eighteenth century. It was characterized by a growing faith in rationalism and science, and a hostility to magic and religion. So it's not surprising that we see a decline of wizards in Western Europe during this period. Nonetheless, not all magicians disappeared. For example the German Franz Mesmer (from whom we get the word "mesmerism") practiced occult healing and attracted a significant following during that time.

Among the most famous wizards of the Enlightenment was the Conte di Cagliostro, a peculiar mixture of visionary, adept, and charlatan.

Born Giuseppe Balsamo in 1743 in Palermo, Italy, he involved himself as a youth in various illegal schemes to cheat people of their money. When he was found out, he fled abroad, where he later claimed to have studied the occult wisdom of the East and learned the arts of alchemy and astrology. Thereafter he adopted the name Cagliostro and traveled throughout Europe peddling his magical skills. He was briefly imprisoned in the Bastille in 1785 on charges of swindling, but was acquitted. He was captured by the Roman Inquisition in 1791 and spent the rest of his life imprisoned in Rome and Montefeltro.

The legendary deeds of Cagliostro were the subject of a number of artistic works. He appears as Sarastro in Mozart's *The Magic Flute* (an opera about, among other things, Freemasonry); in 1875 Johann Strauss wrote an opera entitled *Cagliostro in Wien* (Cagliostro in Vienna). He is also a character (played by Christopher Walken) in the 2001 film *The Affair of the Necklace*, an historically based movie about an event in the 1780s that undermined confidence in the French monarchy.

NINETEENTH-CENTURY WIZARDRY

Wizards practicing their art in the age of Queen Victoria could consult a massive and authoritative history of magic compiled by the industrious French scholar Eliphas Levi (1810–1875), the pen name of Alphonse Louis Constant. Levi studied and systematized the various currents of magic that had been practiced in Europe over the centuries and made them available to ritual magicians. As a result, Paris became an important mecca for wizards who wished to study occult practices.

As well, the nineteenth century saw the emergence of occult groups such as the Rosicrucians, the Theosophists, and the Hermetic Order of the Golden Dawn that drew on the store of magic contained in documents such as the Corpus Hermeticum. Such groups often traced their origins back to the Renaissance or even earlier, to ancient Egypt, the Hebrew Kabbalah, and Eastern mysticism. Madame Helena Blavatsky, the Russian founder of Theosophy, claimed inspiration from the Hermetic writings and from the works of Levi, but she also attributed her ideas to Eastern sources, particularly a group of Indian mystics and wizards called the Mahatmas. Indeed, many wizards and those investigating magical powers began, during the nineteenth and twentieth centuries, to turn their eyes to the East.

In the next chapter, we'll look at wizards who practice their magic in Asia.

CHAPTER 6

———— • ◆ • ————

Wizards of the East

"Those who don't believe in magic
will never find it."

—Roald Dahl, *The Minpins*

lthough we're familiar with some of the great wizards of Western Europe, particularly Merlin, fewer people know about the wizards, sorcerers, and magicians of the time-shrouded lands of Asia and the Middle East. Just as Christianity strongly condemned the use of magic and wizardry in the West, so Islam forbade its practice in the lands that worshipped Allah. Nonetheless, many wizards practiced their trade successfully.

However, magic and wizardry in Eastern legends look considerably different from their Western versions. Certainly we don't find spellcasting men and women in the East wearing long, spangled robes and waving wands. Magical lore in the East often expresses a whimsical character. We can see some of this is in the Chinese story of the Monkey King.

THE MONKEY KING

The tale is part of a larger cycle of Monkey stories that seem to derive from Chinese folklore. They form the basis of the novel *Journey to the West*, written by Wu Cheng'en in the sixteenth century during the Ming Dynasty.

The Monkey King is born from a stone. He wants to be immortal, so he learns many magic spells from a Taoist monk. He can shapeshift, transforming himself into seventy-two different creatures and objects. He can travel on top of the clouds.

In his pride and ambition to gain immortality, he offends the Jade Emperor, the ruler over all heaven and earth. The earth shakes with the sound of their battles, but they reach an impasse and at last the Jade Emperor requests the help of the Buddha. The Buddha drops a mountain on the Monkey King, but it does not kill him, although it renders him immobile. After 500 years he is rescued by several of the Buddha's disciples and together he and his rescuers are sent on a quest to the ultimate West to

bring back to China the sacred Buddhist scriptures. The party has many adventures along the way, helped by the Monkey King/wizard's magical abilities. Finally they complete their quest and return with the sacred sutras, having learned much about each other and about their world.

Monkey King in the Comics

In *Iron Man 2.0* (July 2011), Marvel introduced the character Monkey King. In this version he's a crime lord who models his life after the Monkey King of legend. In addition, several modernized versions of the original story are now available to readers.

Monkey King is certainly not a traditional Western wizard à la Merlin. Although he has magical powers, many of his skills are what we would think of as tricks or illusions. Nonetheless, he is within the wizarding tradition in that some of his powers are genuine.

RUSSIAN WIZARDS

Wizards are often found in the legends of Russia and the Slavic countries. Here we see the more familiar figure of the spell-wielding magician, yet substantial differences still exist from the wizards of the West.

Koschei

Koschei the Deathless is a powerful magic user and a demigod. He lives, as legend says, "beyond twenty-nine countries in the thirtieth country," and is entertained there by a harem of women and a self-playing harp. He is immortal and hides his soul within an egg. Just to make doubly sure it's safe, the egg is inside a duck, which is inside a hare, which is inside an iron chest, which is buried under an oak tree, which is on the island of Bujan.

A Russian fairy tale, "The Death of Koschei the Deathless," tells of a young man who marries a beautiful warrior princess named Marya Morevna. When she goes off to fight in a war, she warns him not to open the door to a certain room in their house. Naturally, the young man immediately does so and finds Koschei, chained up and emaciated. When the young man gives him water, the wizard revives and breaks free, seizing Marya in the process.

The hero pursues him and they fight, but Koschei's powers are too great. The hero is slain and his remains are stuffed in a barrel and tossed in the ocean. Fortunately, Marya's brothers-in-law are powerful wizards and are able to revive him with their own magical powers. To find out how to kill the Deathless, the hero must travel to the hut of the witch Baba Yaga. After passing various tests, the husband is given a magical horse with which he can pursue Koschei. In a final battle, the hero kills Koschei and burns his body.

Koschei the Deathless. An illustration to the fairy tale Marya Morevna by
Ivan Yakovlevich Bilibin (1876–1942)

Koschei's magic is largely focused on death. He often kidnaps women and ransoms them to their husbands. On one occasion he even kidnapped the goddess of death although this didn't turn out well for him, because she persuaded him to tell her the location of his soul—information she passed along to the strapping hero of the story.

Baba Yaga

Another notorious Russian wizard/witch is Baba Yaga, mentioned in the previous story. She lives alone in a hut deep in the forest, surrounded by tangled, forbidding trees. Perhaps the strangest thing about her hut is that it is mounted on two huge chicken legs and can move under her command.

She is tall and thin, with iron teeth and bony arms and legs. Unlike witches and wizards who travel by broom or magic spell, Baba Yaga flies in a giant mortar, crouched in the interior of the bowl.

Baba Yaga, from Vasilisa the Beautiful by Ivan Yakovlevich Bilibin (1876–1942)

The hut itself is extremely frightening, not merely because of its legs but because it is actively malevolent, quite apart from its owner. It will try to crush unwary travellers. It is surrounded, in some accounts, by a fence made of human bones, topped with the skulls of those whom it or its mistress have slain.

In addition to the hut, Baba Yaga is attended by three horsemen, Red, White, and Black, who act as her servants. She also controls several disembodied pairs of hands.

For all her frightening aspects, Baba Yaga has been known to receive and give advice to those who come seeking her services.

Chinese Wizards

Chinese culture has a rich tradition of folklore, going back many thousands of years. Not surprisingly, this tradition includes many examples of wizardry. Especially popular is the shamanistic tradition of second sight and divination. Wizards, the Chinese believed, were possessed by the gods and imbued with a magical power to speak in the gods' names. Often they served not merely as foretellers of the future but as exorcists and political counselors.

Wu and Yi

Wizardry and shamanism have a long and complex evolution in China. Some scholars separate the Chinese shamanic tradition from that of Siberian shamans. However, it seems clear that the two have many points in common.

Sometimes, this could be dangerous. Zhang Liang was a government official during the Tang Dynasty (618–907), and a powerful advisor to the Tang rulers. However, among the people with whom he surrounded himself were two sorcerers, Cheng Gongying and Gongsun Chang. They suggested that Zhang himself was destined to occupy the imperial throne—a dangerous thought that could easily lead to disaster. Sure enough, word of this got back to the emperor, who ordered an investigation into the matter. Zheng's enemies at court took the opportunity to gain their revenge on him, and he was executed in 646, along with one of the wizards.

Healers, Rainmakers, and Dream Interpreters

Chinese shamans also practiced healing; the word *wu*, meaning shaman, was sometimes combined with *yi*, healing, to form *wuyi*. As part of this responsibility, the wizards also performed exorcisms. On occasion, they would run shrieking through the streets, brandishing spears in an effort to drive out evil spirits. Prisoners (that is, humans suspected of being possessed by evil spirits) would be taken out of the city gates and publically dismembered as a warning to any recalcitrant demons who refused to allow the wizards to expel them.

Some wizards also possessed the power to affect rainfall, an essential quality in any agricultural community. Wizards would dance within a ring of fire, chanting and occasionally tossing sacred objects into the flames. Their own sweat, it was said, was the essential magic that produced the needed raindrops.

Interpreters of Dreams

Still other wizards practiced oneiromancy, or the interpretation of dreams. In one notable instance, a wizard interpreted the dream of a lord who had dreamed of a demon. The demon, according to the wizard, represented the Zhao family, two of whose members the lord had unjustly slain. The meaning of the dream, the wizard informed the lord, was that the lord would not taste "new wheat"—that is, he would be dead within a short time.

Shortly afterword, new wheat was brought before the lord to taste. Contemptuous of his wizard's prediction, the lord made to take a bite of the wheat but was suddenly struck with an urge to go to the privy. While there, he tumbled in and died, fulfilling the wizard's prediction.

Some wizards seem to have risen to important positions at court, though this was potentially perilous if their predictions did not come true or if, in the eyes of the emperor, they predicted an inconvenient future. Even today in remote parts of China, as well as in other areas of Asia, the figure of the local shaman, wizard, or witchdoctor, clad in colorful costume, including numerous bells to drive away evil spirits, is common.

 ## MANGA WIZARDS

One of the most popular literary forms in contemporary Japan is *manga*—comics. In recent years, they've spread from Japan to the United States and Europe, making popular the "anime" style of drawing. Many manga comics have been translated into English and have been the basis for popular television cartoon shows (including the biggest property of all some years ago, Pokémon). As well, some popular American novels have been translated into Japanese and published as mangas (for example, James Patterson's Witch & Wizard series).

Many—though not all—manga deal with magic and wizards. Among these are:

- *Yu-Gi-Oh*
- *Howl's Moving Castle*
- *Witchblade*
- *Nausicaä of the Valley of the Wind*
- *Magic Knight Rayearth*
- *Negima!*

Negima! is typical of these stories. Written by Ken Akamatsu, it focuses on Negi, a young Welsh wizard who wants to become a master of magic. He graduates from the Welsh Meridiana Magic Academy and travels to Japan, where he becomes an English teacher. Although intimidated by teaching and impatient with the limited opportunities, as he sees it, to use his magical abilities, he gradually comes to recognize the importance of what he is doing. Using his powers, he is able to help his students with their problems and grow in skills as well as maturity.

Akamatsu's wizards use a system of magic that involves two people acting in concert: the magician and someone else. They enter into a *pactio*, wherein the wizard transfers some of his power to the other person. The wizard creates two cards as a symbol of the pact, giving one to the other person and keeping one for himself. The cards allow the two to magically communicate and permit the wizard to enhance the other person's powers.

An anime series based on the manga aired in Japan in 2005, followed by a second series that aired in 2006.

Manga and Anime

People occasionally conflate the terms "manga" and "anime"; they are, in fact, two different things. Manga refers to comics and cartooning. In particular, it refers to the comics that are ubiquitous throughout Japan. Anime, although it is sometimes also used to refer to Japanese animated cartoons, is more particularly applied to their drawing style.

Another notable contribution to comic book wizards from the manga tradition is Lina Inverse from the Slayers series. She is a young and powerful sorceress who dubs herself a "magical genius." Lina specializes in black magic with a touch of shamanism and white magic, in addition to having some skill as a swordswoman. She has an extremely high magic capacity and is able to draw upon incredibly destructive spells such as the Ragna Blade and Giga Slave. The Slayer franchise originated in a series of novels that were later adapted into manga, televised anime series, anime films, roleplaying video games, and other media.

In all, traditions of the wizard are not as developed in the East as in the West. What is primarily emphasized in Asian cultures are the shamanistic aspects of wizardry: the ability to foretell the future, to heal, to drive out demons, and so forth.

We now turn to the legends of wizards that mark our continuing interest in these strange, ethereal figures.

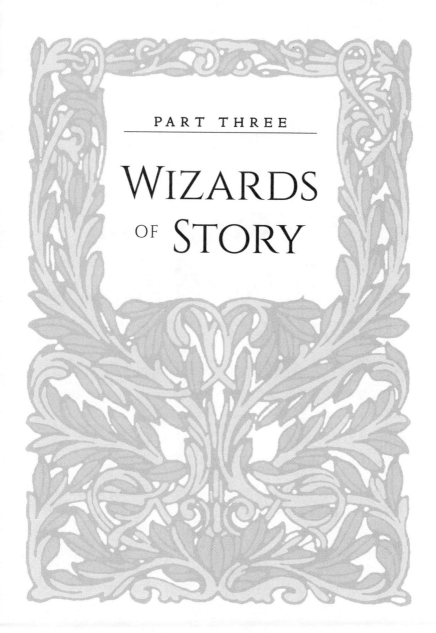

PART THREE

WIZARDS OF STORY

CHAPTER 7

The Wizards of Harry Potter

"You're a wizard, Harry."

—Hagrid, *Harry Potter and the Sorcerer's Stone* by J.K. Rowling

f all wizards who are part of the popular imagination today, none has attracted more interest or excitement than a small, dark-haired boy with glasses and a strange lightning-bolt-shaped scar on his forehead. It seems appropriate, therefore, to begin our investigation of wizards in popular literature and on screen with one whose fame has swept the globe: Harry Potter.

Few literary works have spawned such a web of influence as J.K. Rowling's Harry Potter series. Seven novels of ever-increasing page

count and eight films of ever-increasing budgets released over thirteen years; multiple companion books, ancillary works and spin-offs, video games and merchandise, countless fan websites and wikis. Certainly, there are other fantasy works that use more words with longer publication timelines—Robert Jordan's meandering Wheel of Time series comes to mind—but there's something about Harry Potter that has grabbed our collective consciousness in a way that few things have before. Doubtless, Rowling's creation will echo through the pop culture world of this century and beyond. Any book about wizards would be incomplete without a discussion of the Harry Potter phenomenon.

J.K. Rowling's accomplishment is a type of wizardry in its own right. Harry Potter has become the best-selling book series in history, moving more that 400 million copies worldwide. The stories became the basis for a series of blockbuster movies that, in turn, became the highest-grossing film series in history. The change in Rowling's own life was nothing short of magical. In the decade following the 1998 publication of *Harry Potter and the Philosopher's Stone,* (the original British title for *Harry Potter and the Sorcerer's* Stone) she went from living on state benefits to amassing a fortune estimated at $798 million. She is the United Kingdom's best-selling author with sales in excess of $398 million. In the year of publication of the final Harry Potter book, *TIME* magazine named her as a runner-up for its 2007 Person of the Year, and the National Magazine Company named her "Most Influential Woman in Britain" in 2010. To say the Potter franchise was a success for Rowling is something of an understatement.

HARRY, HERMIONE, AND RON

Of course, much of the appeal has to do with Rowling's detailed story-telling and portrayal of the characters. At the heart of the Potter world is the trio of wizards we've seen grow up before our eyes: Harry Potter, Hermione Granger, and Ron Weasley. All born with the ability to be wizards, they are sent to Hogwarts School of Witchcraft and Wizardry for proper training. The three are cast as misfits—Harry has the burden of a fame he doesn't understand, Hermione is portrayed as a know-it-all bookworm, and Ron, as the youngest male Weasley, has a long wizarding tradition to uphold—and they become fast friends. At school, they uncover nefarious plots to reincarnate the dark wizard Voldemort, plots that become deeper and darker as the series continues. As a team they complement each other: Harry is the man of action tempered by Hermione's cool calculations, and Ron is the emotional center.

Anchored in the young-adult literary genre, the books are also full of relatable teen angst as the three characters navigate the complexities of school dances and secret crushes, all while attempting to save the world. The focus at the center of the story is one of personal interaction: love, revenge, the lust for power, and redemption—wizardry is just the backdrop against which all this unfolds. And ultimately, the Harry Potter series follows only a sketch of the wizarding traditions we're exploring in this book.

The accessibility of Rowling's characters is also enhanced by her decision to set the wizarding world in the midst of the mundane. Despite the presence of magic, Harry Potter's universe often mirrors the tedium and fussy bureaucracy of non-magical society. It's a nod to the common ancestry of wizard and Muggle types, and a suggestion that Harry's fantastic realm is only a sidestep away. When the characters transition from school robes to street clothes, and we start seeing Harry and crew in coffee shops, we get a strong sense that these wizards are really living *in* the world. But in truth they are apart from it, often right under the noses of Muggles.

> "The wizards represent all that the true 'Muggle' most fears: They are plainly outcasts and comfortable with being so. Nothing is more unnerving to the truly conventional than the unashamed misfit!"
>
> —J.K. ROWLING

Everyday people pass by the telephone box that leads to the Ministry of Magic without a hint of what goes on below it. Londoners might stroll past the Leaky Cauldron without any idea that out back the center of wizarding commerce in the British Isles, Diagon Alley, hums with activity. Our non-magical world is kept at bay through the use of charms, spells, and secrecy: It is strictly forbidden to reveal anything about magic to Muggle society. However, we learn in *Harry Potter and the Half-Blood Prince* that the Muggle prime minister has traditionally been made aware of the wizarding world, primarily to collude with the Ministry of Magic to cover up incidents where the machinations of wizards intrude into the ordinary.

> "By the way, the Harry Potter series is literature, in spite of what some people might say. The way J.K. Rowling worked that world out is quite something."
>
> —GARY OLDMAN

The pop culture saturation resulting from seven books and eight movies being released regularly, sometimes simultaneously, for almost fifteen years, fueled the Potter phenomenon. Typing "Harry Potter" into a Google search bar will return more than 200 million hits: It's hard to escape or deny that level of ubiquity. The films, in particular, have created a collective imagery for us to access that increases the franchise's pop-culture presence. Indeed, the films are wholly tied into the books now—Harry Potter can't look like anyone but Daniel Radcliffe.

But where does Rowling's depiction of wizardry place in the larger wizarding tradition we've been exploring in this book? Many of the images are familiar: Wizards sport robes and wands; potent incantations abound. Broomsticks or flying cars and motorcycles serve as a means of transportation. Charmed objects such as the remembrall and the time-turner are useful tools of the trade. Rowling's wizards are a blend of traditions, but her take on magic has its unique elements.

Using Magic in the Potterverse

On his or her eleventh birthday, a British child with wizarding ability is sent a letter explaining that he or she has been accepted into Hogwarts School of Witchcraft and Wizardry. Education must be completed there for the students to be considered mature and capable members of wizarding society. The wizarding ability is inborn, akin to a genetic mutation that can manifest or remain dormant and is passed from parents to offspring. Even if the so-called "wizarding gene" does not manifest, it still remains in the blood as a recessive trait. This results in the occasional wizard or witch, such as Hermione Granger, being Muggle-born. It is assumed that a squib—a non-wizard born to wizard parents—must have married into Hermione's family line at some time in the past.

Wizards International

As we discover in *Harry Potter and the Goblet of Fire*, Hogwarts is not the only wizarding school. There are at least two others: Beauxbatons in France and Durmstrang in Scandinavia. As far as can be determined from the book, Beauxbatons attracts students from French-speaking countries, whereas Durmstrang takes in students from Northern and Eastern Europe and Russia. Curiously, there is no mention of Asian schools of wizardry, although presumably they exist.

Other beings in the Potter world (or the Potterverse, as it's sometimes called by devotees) can also perform magic, such as house elves and goblins. The Forbidden Forest is filled with magical creatures, including centaurs and unicorns, as well as giant spiders, and Hagrid,

Keeper of Keys and Grounds, generally knows where to find them. There are malicious creatures in those dark woods certainly, but Hagrid continually reminds us that some are just misunderstood.

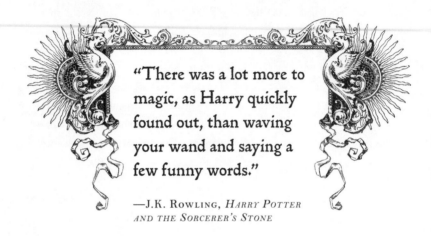

"There was a lot more to magic, as Harry quickly found out, than waving your wand and saying a few funny words."

—J.K. ROWLING, *HARRY POTTER AND THE SORCERER'S STONE*

House Elves

House elves have their own brand of magic, as do many other magical creatures. Their magic allows them to perform unique tasks, such as "apparating" (teleporting from one place to another) where wizards normally cannot. The house-elf is bound by an unspecified contract to its master and can be freed if given a piece of clothing. (This is how Harry separates Dobby the house-elf from the Malfoy family.) A house-elf is incredibly powerful but hobbled by his subservient nature. To have a house-elf is to own him wholly, and he is loathe to commit sins against his master.

Interestingly, the magic of house elves is quite different from— and in some respects more powerful than—that exercised by wizards.

Dobby not only defends Harry from an attack by Lucius Malfoy; he blasts his former master off his feet with a gesture (house elves don't use wands). It's also worth noting that although Rowling has said that house elves' rights improve after Hermione joins the Ministry of Magic after leaving Hogwarts, the fundamental fact of their wizardly enslavement remains unchanged (as far as we know) at the end of the series.

 ## THE MAGIC OF THE POTTERVERSE

Magic in Harry Potter's world uses the classic combination of words, gestures, and magic wands (material components such as herbs aren't generally required for Hogwarts' spells, though they are for potions). It makes some sense that magic words are mostly Latin and pseudo-Latin, given that the wizarding world is rooted in the Western world, (one wonders what magical incantations would sound like in the Chinese equivalent of Hogwarts), but the incantations and charms border on bizarre at times. Luna Lovegood employs a charm to turn ears to kumquats, and the incantation *Vera Verto!* (and the proper wave of a wand) will change an animal into a water goblet.

Spells are the everyday tools of a wizard. Typically, casting requires an incantation, but sufficiently advanced wizards can perform spells without words. Although most spells used in the Potter books require the caster to use his or her voice, some spells can be cast nonverbally. A wand may still be required, although animagi (wizards with the ability to change themselves into animals), for example, do not need wands to undergo their transformations. It is also possible to use a wand without holding it. Harry performs *Lumos!* to light his wand when it is lying on the ground near him.

"The spells are made up. I have met people who assure me, very seriously, that they are trying to do them, and I can assure them, just as seriously, that they don't work."

—J.K. ROWLING

Wands are very important to a wizard in Harry's world. In the Potterverse, the wand is said to choose its owner, which suggests a mystical connection, but here—as in real-life wizardry—the wand is largely utilitarian. It is an instrument through which a wizard can focus her or his magical powers for results. Spells can be cast without the use of wands, utilizing keen concentration and skill. A wand, though, is a highly personal object; Harry feels a strong sense of familiarity and relief when he grasps his own wand toward the end of *Harry Potter and the Deathly Hallows.*

Wands are just one among many objects imbued with magic in the world of Harry Potter. The remembrall is a tennis ball–sized ball made of glass that contains smoke that turns red when its owner has forgotten something. The time-turner is a necklace shaped like an hourglass that is capable of transporting the wearer through time. The number of times one turns the hourglass corresponds to the number of hours one travels back in time. Other magical objects include mirrors, quills, books, and everyday objects such as newspapers and paintings—anything can be enchanted with magic.

The Elder Wand

One of the fabled Deathly Hallows, the Elder Wand is Voldemort's object of pursuit; it said to have been bestowed on the wizard Antioch Peverell by Death himself. If brought together with the other two Hallows—the Resurrection Stone and the Cloak of Invisibility—the wielder will become the Master of Death.

It is worth noting how magic evolves as the series progresses. In the first book, magic is largely a curiosity; the young wizards learn to use and control it, but they can't do much with it, perhaps because they do not have extensive experience yet. By the end, though, they've become masters of magic—especially Hermione. Magic can send people into the spirit world and bring them back again. It can create a defensive barrier as well as attack fellow wizards. The range of available spells seems endless—confirming that in the Potterverse, magic is technology (consider that Mrs. Weasley uses what amounts to a magical dishwasher).

Compare this with Tolkien's Gandalf. The old wizard rarely uses spells at all (once, when the party is battling a monster in the Mines of Moria), and when he does the reader expects something grand to happen.

Harry Potter's world uses magic like we use electricity or the Internet. Hogwarts doesn't have computers—naturally, because the school is not wired for electricity—but also because wizards just don't have a need for it. Enchanted quills write your dictation; owls deliver news right to you; enchanted chess pieces play out a match before your eyes. Magic functions as technology, and it can do almost anything. To a point, it seems Rowling is making it up as she goes along: If you missed the invisible train to Hogwarts, there's a flying car you can take. Or perhaps a friendly wizard will just teleport you there. Magic here is a great convenience for a wizard.

Spells are divided into rough categories such as charms and jinxes. There are, apparently, hundreds of spells, and the series gives us a glimpse of just a small sample. The use of malicious spells, such as curses and hexes, is considered improper. A dark wizard generally employs such improper spells without compunction. Hogwarts exists to teach not just the mechanics of spells but also the ethical use of magic.

Here is a list of some of the major wizarding spells used by Harry and his friends and associates:

- *Avada Kedavra: Killing Curse*: Causes instant, painless death. There is no way to block this spell, which makes it one of the three Unforgivable Curses, along with *Crucio* (the Cruciatus Curse, used to torture people) and *Imperio* (the Imperius Curse, employed for mind control). Only two people in the history of the magical world are known to have survived the killing curse: Harry Potter and Voldemort. Because these unforgivable curses are very powerful, they require great skill and willpower to use.

- *Stupefy: Stunning Charm*: Used extensively by the forces of Hogwarts during their battles with the Death Eaters in *Harry Potter and the Deathly Hallows*, it is the basic spell for fighting between wizards.

- *Reducto: Reductor Curse*: Enables the spellcaster to explode solid objects. Harry uses it on one of the hedges of the Triwizard maze in *Harry Potter and the Goblet of Fire*. Students practice with it while training in Dumbledore's Army, the secret student organization formed in *Harry Potter and the Order of the Phoenix.*

- *Accio: Summoning Charm*: First mentioned in *Harry Potter and the Goblet of Fire,* this charm summons an object to the caster. Near the end of the book, Harry uses it to summon the Triwizard Cup after he encounters Voldemort.

- *Alohomora: Unlocking Charm*: Opens or unlocks doors. Used throughout the series, appearing first in *Harry Potter and the Sorcerer's Stone.* Rowling has said that the word's origin is from a West African Sidiki dialect with the literal meaning "friendly to thieves."

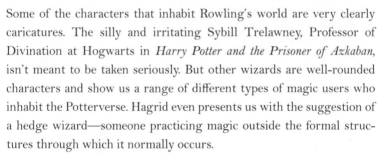

WIZARDKIND

Some of the characters that inhabit Rowling's world are very clearly caricatures. The silly and irritating Sybill Trelawney, Professor of Divination at Hogwarts in *Harry Potter and the Prisoner of Azkaban,* isn't meant to be taken seriously. But other wizards are well-rounded characters and show us a range of different types of magic users who inhabit the Potterverse. Hagrid even presents us with the suggestion of a hedge wizard—someone practicing magic outside the formal structures through which it normally occurs.

Let's look at some of the wizard types Rowling shows us.

Harry Potter

As Harry is the figure at the center of the story, it's no surprise that his influence on the world rises to the level of a thaumaturgist, although his wonderworking is still developing throughout the series. He's an accomplished magician by the time of his final battle with Voldemort, although not surprisingly his specialty is battle magic. This comes in handy when the students of Hogwarts form a secret army, Dumbledore's Army, and Harry begins to train them in fighting dark magic.

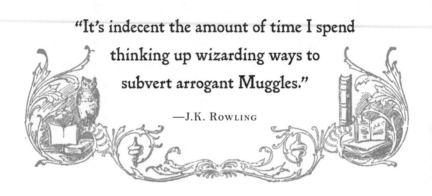

> "It's indecent the amount of time I spend thinking up wizarding ways to subvert arrogant Muggles."
>
> —J.K. ROWLING

Harry's role in the story is that of a messiah: subject of prophecy, savior, and the mirror to Lord Voldemort. He is the Chosen One, appointed by destiny to clash with the greatest dark wizard of all time. He can speak Parseltongue, a skill normally reserved for dark wizards. He is also is able to evoke a very powerful patronus charm; not all wizards can do this, and some can only do it partially. The patronus is a manifestation of the self, a spirit guardian conjured in times of great need.

Albus Dumbledore

At the beginning of the saga, Dumbledore seems similar to T.H. White's Merlin: a mild, pleasant, bumbling spellcaster. However, he evolves over the course of the series to be come a formidable tactician with a subtle endgame. He inhabits the role of the sage or magus quite comfortably. Dumbledore is portrayed as a master of charms that affect the mind, and like Merlin, he is able to prophesy. Dumbledore does not use aggressive magic as much as other wizards, which is consistent with a character who believes that power derives from the quality of one's soul and not the quantity of one's spells.

Severus Snape

The half-blood prince's aptitude for potions suggests Snape's affinity for alchemy. He is the secretive dark master laboring in his laboratory over his cauldrons, retorts, and hissing beakers down in the bowels of the castle. Interestingly, Snape's power is not as overt as some of the other wizards' in Harry Potter's world. Potions are a more subtle form of magic, and in several places Rowling suggests that this is precisely what attracts Snape to them. Perhaps the alchemists of history were just as likely to be covert in their use of magic. Another famous alchemist, Nicholas Flamel—still alive in Harry's world—makes an appearance as the creator of the sorcerer's stone in the series' first book.

Sirius Black

Sirius Black has an ability few other wizards in the Potterverse have managed to master. He is an animagus, although unregistered. (All animagi are required to register with the Ministry of Magic.) His ability to transform into a massive black dog evokes the shamanistic practice of shapeshifting. (It's worth noting that Sirius is often referred to as the "Dog Star.") The shaman troupe is reinforced by Sirius's role as Harry's godfather and mentor. He even finds a way to manipulate the elements to make his face appear in the burning coals of a fireplace to speak with Harry in *Harry Potter and the Goblet of Fire*. Sirius has shades of the mystic much more than other wizards.

Shapeshifting Wizards

An animagus is a wizard who can transform him- or herself into an animal at will without a wand or an incantation. It is a learned transfiguration, rather than a hereditary skill or a blood infection like lycanthropy: The wizard still retains a sense of self and human thought process, though simplified. Animagi in the Potter world include Minerva McGonagall, Peter Pettigrew, and Rita Skeeter. All animagi are required to register with the Ministry of Magic at the Improper Use of Magic Office, and specify their animal forms and distinguishing markings.

DARK WIZARDS

As in all realms, the Potterverse has its share of wizards who are tempted by power. Wizards who have joined the cause of Voldemort are known as Death Eaters and are wholly owned by him. The members of the inner circle have Dark Marks—a winding snake exiting the mouth of a skull—burned into their left forearms that compel them to teleport to Voldemort's side on command. This group of wizards holds many pureblood supremacists who practiced the Dark Arts. They are Voldemort's masked army, striking fear into the hearts of ordinary wizards; their names are whispered in hushed tones on the shadowed ways of Diagon Alley.

Voldemort

Tom Riddle became the sorcerer Voldemort, Master of Death. Skilled in necromancy, he has split his soul into pieces and tied them to horcruxes. He's then scattered these powerful charms so death can never truly find him. A classic villain who sees his machinations as the way to bring order to the world, he is, in many respects, a fallen angel. His followers do not hesitate to use taboo rituals in the service of his resurrection. Voldemort has caused such fear in the wizarding community that it is considered an ill omen to speak his name aloud.

What Is a Horcrux?

A devious method to confuse death, the horcrux is a powerful object in which a dark wizard has hidden a fragment of his or her soul. Thereby, the soul is anchored to the earth should the wizard's corporeal form be destroyed. Functionally, a wizard employing such charms can attain immortality. More than one horcrux can pull on a soul, straining it; the cost is diminished humanity and even physical disfigurement.

Bellatrix Lestrange

Bellatrix is a particularly nasty, though powerful, witch. A pure-blood who became a Death Eater upon her graduation from Hogwarts, she is fanatically loyal to Voldemort. Bellatrix is one of the few known female Death Eaters, and also one of the most ruthless. She is responsible for the deaths of Sirius Black, Nymphadora Tonks, and the house-elf Dobby. She nearly killed Harry and held Hermione at knifepoint. At the final battle at Hogwarts, Bellatrix fights Hermione Granger, Ginny Weasley, and Luna Lovegood all at once, and the three young witches still cannot equal Bellatrix's magical abilities. A mother's rage proves stronger than a witch's wand, however, when Molly Weasley, enraged by a near-fatal attack on her daughter and the death of her son, defeats Bellatrix once and for all.

Lucius Malfoy

Death Eater Lucius Malfoy II is a pureblood wizard, the father of Draco Malfoy, Harry's nemesis at Hogwarts. An aristocratic wizard of ancient lineage, he believes strongly in notions of blood purity and the superiority of pureblood wizards; this makes Lucius a natural fit for Slytherin House, whose students are generally more concerned about these matters than others at Hogwarts. Lucius is a moderately accomplished wizard who plays with forces beyond his control. By the end of the series, he has fallen out of favor with the Dark Lord and is treated as little more than a servant, eventually renouncing Voldemort to save himself and his family.

Draco Malfoy

Draco Malfoy, Lucius's son and heir, is Harry's arch nemesis, and the bully of the Hogwarts schoolyard. Draco probably does worse than a common bully in that he actually consorts with Death Eaters and plots to murder his headmaster with his dad's crazy friends. In the films,

Tom Felton's snide deliveries of "Potter" made you love to hate Draco. He's a foil for Harry and represents ideas of privilege and pureblood wizarding that Harry opposes. But there is also a conflicted side to Draco, and the reader is led to think he's being dragged over to the dark side rather than going willingly. This is confirmed in the story's epilogue, when we see an older, sadder, and perhaps wiser Draco sending his son off to his first year at Hogwarts.

Purebloods

A theme that runs through the Harry Potter series is the notion, popular among some wizards, that as magical folk they are innately superior to Muggles. From this there flows the belief that the best wizards are those who come from families with no (or very little) Muggle blood in them. This idea, similar to Nazi doctrines about pure Germanic/Aryan stock, is at the heart of Voldemort's attempt to seize power in the wizarding world.

The dark side is clearly defined in Rowling's wizarding world, but there are occasionally shades of gray. For example, wizards make use of the creatures known as Dementors to serve as guards at the wizarding prison. This is at least partly because Dementors are considered one of the most dangerous creatures in the world. They feed off human happiness, wearing depression and despair like a cloak. There is no compromise with a Dementor and the most effective defense against it is to evoke the patronus charm: a spell rooted in the spirit and goodwill of the caster. As Professor Lupin tells Harry:

"Dementors are among the foulest creatures that walk this earth. They infest the darkest, filthiest places, they glory in decay and despair, they drain peace, hope, and happiness out of the air around them . . . Get too near a Dementor and every good feeling, every happy memory will be sucked out of you. If it can, the Dementor will feed on you long enough to reduce you to something like itself—soulless and evil. You will be left with nothing but the worst experiences of your life."

This being the case, we're left with the question of why wizards would make any use of such creatures at all. The answer is that they find it expedient to do so. Wizards in the wizarding government aren't that different from Muggle politicians—they make compromises and protect themselves above all else. The use of Dementors represents such a compromise.

Aurors in the Potterverse

An Auror investigates crimes related to the Dark Arts and apprehends dark wizards. This makes them, essentially, a wizarding police force. Auror training is very difficult and intensive. Rowling's online comments after she finished writing the saga are to the effect that Harry became the youngest Auror in history, and then rose to the position of Head Auror. Rowling's term seems to be a blend of "aura" and "augur," as in, a detective who listens for extrasensory clues to unravel a mystery.

WITCHES AND WIZARDS

A true witch might take issue with the portrayal of the witch in the Harry Potter stories. Despite the name of Hogwarts School of Witchcraft and Wizardry, which implies the two are distinct and equal disciplines, witchcraft is largely folded into wizardry without much distinction made between the two.

The term "witchcraft" refers to the practice of magic, as does wizardry. Both males and females may be called witches or wizards. The term "warlock," although sometimes incorrectly believed to mean a male witch, is really an Old English term for liar or oath breaker.

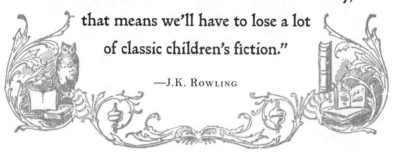

"I think the Harry books are very moral, but some people just object to witchcraft being mentioned in a children's book. Unfortunately, that means we'll have to lose a lot of classic children's fiction."

—J.K. ROWLING

"Warlock" is rarely used in Harry Potter's wizarding world—perhaps for good reason. It sometimes is used to describe an unusually fierce male wizard or as a title denoting particular skill or achievement, similar to a Muggle being knighted. In Harry's world, it denoted someone skilled in magical dueling or was given as a title to a wizard who had preformed feats of bravery. Albus Dumbledore, himself, is former Chief Warlock of the Wizengamot, the Potterverse's high law court. A fierce warlock is the protaganist of "The Warlock's Hairy Heart," a tale mentioned briefly by Dumbledore and later penned by Rowling in *The Tales of Beedle the Bard*, a volume she published after completing the Potter series.

Both witches and wizards ride brooms in Harry's world to play Quidditch; we aren't shown any other instances of the students at Hogwarts riding brooms, with the notable exception of the Triwizard Tournament in *Harry Potter and the Goblet of Fire*. Rowling's witches are strong women and role models with whom her young-adult audience can identify. And as in *The Wonderful Wizard of Oz*, some witches are good and some are wicked.

WIZARDING SCHOOL

"There will be no foolish wand-waving or silly incantations in this class. As such, I don't expect many of you to appreciate the subtle science and exact art that is potion-making. However, for those select few who possess the predisposition . . . I can teach you how to bewitch the mind and ensnare the senses. I can tell you how to bottle fame, brew glory, and even put a stopper in death."

—SEVERUS SNAPE IN THE FILM *HARRY POTTER AND THE SORCERER'S STONE*

Modeled after the British public school, Hogwarts is central to the Harry Potter universe. All the wizards and witches of the United Kingdom have filtered through Hogwarts at one time or another. Indeed, the learning of magic rises to the level of standardized testing at Hogwarts, which makes it all the more like high school with magic. Who hasn't fussed over exams the same way Hermione does? Who cannot help but cringe at the thought of Severus Snape leering over one's shoulder like a disapproving chemistry teacher?

In Britain the words "public schools" refer to private independent schools in the United Kingdom. They are called public schools because there is no extracurricular affiliation to a religious institution or similar restrictive body. Historically, they have educated the sons of the English upper and upper-middle classes, and have sometimes been jokingly compared to prisons by former students. Hogwarts's imposing walls may evoke a cold, dark prison—particularly perched on the overcast moors of Scotland—but the school is certainly a warmer place than that.

To advance through the wizarding educational system, students at Hogwarts must attend certain classes and pass exams with clever-sounding acronyms. Ordinary Wizarding Level (abbreviated O.W.L.) is a subject-specific test taken during fifth year. Regulated by the Wizarding Examinations Authority, the test functions as a basic equivalency test where the score determines whether or not a wizard will be allowed to continue taking that subject in subsequent years. A Nastily Exhausting Wizarding Test (often abbreviated N.E.W.T.) is a subject-specific exam that seventh-year students take to help them pursue certain careers after their graduation. Only Auror applicants with at least five N.E.W.T.s with top grades of either "Exceeds Expectations" or "Outstanding" need apply to the Ministry of Magic. Anti-cheating quills and anti-cheating spells are commonly employed during the tests to prevent academic dishonesty.

O.W.L.s and N.E.W.T.s

The O.W.L. and N.E.W.T. are clearly inspired by the old British Ordinary Level (O-level) and Advanced Level (A-level) exams that Rowling herself most certainly had to suffer through. American readers can think of them as comparable to the SATs.

Just as at public schools such as Eton or Harrow, students at Hogwarts are organized into houses—although here it's done by the mystical Sorting Hat: Gryffindor, Ravenclaw, Hufflepuff, or Slytherin House.

(Rowling foreshadows Harry's unexpected ties to Voldemort when the Sorting Hat suggests that Harry could be a candidate for Slytherin House.) Each student wears robes as a uniform and sports ties and scarves in their house colors, which contributes to a sense of community.

"I don't believe in witchcraft, though I've lost count of the number of times I've been told I'm a practicing witch. Ninety—let's say ninety-five percent at least, of the magic in the books is entirely invented by me. And I've used things from folklore and I've used bits of what people used to believe worked magically just to add a certain flavor, but I've always twisted them to suit my own ends. I mean, I've taken liberties with folklore to suit my plot."

—J.K. ROWLING

House Points

House points are awarded to students at Hogwarts who do good deeds or correctly answer questions in class. They can also be taken away for rule-breaking. The points are stored in house-point hourglasses. Each student earns points for his or her house, and at the end of the year, the house with the most points is awarded the house cup.

HARRY'S ALLIES

Fortunately, as Dumbledore informs Harry, "help will always be given at Hogwarts to those who ask for it." Despite the perils he faces, Harry has plenty of help in combatting them.

Minerva McGonagall

Professor Minerva McGonagall, the head of Gryffindor House, is a guiding force throughout the series. She keeps a watchful eye on Harry and his friends, and intervenes on their behalf whenever necessary. She is there at the beginning when Harry is placed on the Dursleys's doorstep, and she is there at the end organizing the resistance to Voldemort at the final battle of Hogwarts. Her wit is pointed and quick in the great tradition of an English headmistress. Professor McGonagall does not suffer fools lightly, but there is warmth and caring underneath her strict demeanor. As a registered animagus, she is particularly skilled at transfiguration, and is a powerful witch in her own right. During the Battle of Hogwarts, she is able to fend off many dark wizards and can even hold off Voldemort for a time. Like a mother bear's, her wrath is great when roused.

Neville Longbottom

Although he appears clumsy and not particularly bright at first, Neville Longbottom has a compelling story arc. The nerdy kid who's good with plants ultimately gets to wield the sword of Godric Gryffindor and destroy the seventh and final horcrux. Sorted with Harry and Ron in their first year, Neville is initially shy and clumsy. However, he becomes an important member of Dumbledore's Army—Harry's secret collection of dissidents on the side of good—and fights in all the battles of the

Second Wizarding War. Later, Neville takes a position as professor of Herbology at Hogwarts, having always had an affinity for making magic with herbs.

Hagrid, Keeper of Keys and Grounds

The first friend of Harry Potter, the half-giant Rubeus Hagrid is an amiable, rough-hewn, charming—and occasionally dangerous—character. Framed for a crime he did not commit, he was expelled from Hogwarts and forbidden from doing magic. Dumbledore managed to intervene and secure him a position as groundskeeper of Hogwarts. He is very loyal to his friends and is ready to defend them or fight for them if necessary. Hagrid has a great love of magical creatures, and is more comfortable among the denizens of the Forbidden Forest than anywhere else. He may remind us of a hedge wizard, with his umbrella standing in for a wand, but Hagrid is quite skilled in the use of magic. Unfortunately, his fondness for magical pets leads him to adopt a baby dragon and befriend a giant spider, as well as assign students an apparently homicidal book about caring for magical creatures.

Luna Lovegood

Luna Lovegood has a quirky vibe, and seems able to see beyond the ordinary. Her mother passed when Luna was young, and her father, editor of the *Quibbler* magazine, raised her. First appearing in *Harry Potter and the Order of the Phoenix*, Luna was sorted into Ravenclaw House and joins Dumbledore's Army in her fourth year. Because of her father's political position at the time, Luna is abducted by Death Eaters to be held ransom and imprisoned in Malfoy Manor. She is freed by Dobby the house-elf, and eventually returns to Hogwarts to participate in the final battles.

Ginny Weasley

Ginevra Weasley is youngest of Arthur and Molly Weasley's seven children, the only female born into the Weasley clan. A star-stuck preteen around Harry initially, she evolves into a valuable member of Dumbledore's Army and a love interest for Harry. During her first year at Hogwarts, she came under the influence of the memory of Tom Riddle's sixteen-year-old self, preserved in a diary, and was forced to reopen the Chamber of Secrets. Since that time she has been continually pulled into the orbit of Harry Potter.

THE POTTERVERSE

Ultimately, we come back to the question of why Harry Potter is so popular. Although the fans of Harry Potter are legion, the praise for Rowling's work is by no means universal. The venerable writer Ursula K. Le Guin has commented that Rowling's work is "good fare for its age group, but stylistically ordinary, imaginatively derivative, and ethically rather mean-spirited." Other critics have pointed out the numerous plot holes and, at times, the incomprehensible actions of the characters. Nevertheless, the books have sold phenomenally and fans have stuck with the series even at the low points. There's a certain level of psychological investment once a reader gets three or four volumes in, and just from the sheer volume of media exposure the series received, readers can't help but garner some interest in it. Moreover, the stars of the film become like those distant cousins you only see on holidays as you watch them mature from children to young adults on screen.

Yet, there must be something in these stories that hooks people initially. The curiosity of a wizarding school explains part of it: Harry,

Hermione, and Ron are just like us—except they study magic. Mix in a compelling mystery and some interpersonal conflicts, and we're very close to any Muggle secondary school. British readers would be amused by the typical public-school system being turned on its head by charms and spells. And for the American reader, the Dickensian ring of names like Flitwick, Crookshanks, and Longbottom add an exotic flavor on top of the magic that infuses everything.

Rowling's naming conventions lend a lot of the so-called British charm to the Potter world. But her technique is also a deft literary device employed to give us a succinct impression of these characters. Professor Sprout is the botany professor; Professor Flitwick is small and fragile. It's an example of Rowling's thoroughly detailed imagined world for which she has garnered much praise. Yet, Rowling's world didn't come to American audiences unfiltered. The first book in the series was published as *Harry Potter and the Philosopher's Stone* in the United Kingdom, but fearing the title a bit obscure for American audiences, Scholastic asked Rowling to change the title to *Sorcerer's Stone*. There are other instances of "translation" between the two dialects of English. Hermione says, "gets off with" and it had to be changed to "go on a date with."

Beyond the quirks of the cultures on either side of the pond, Harry Potter as literature taps into strong emotions and classic motifs. Harry and his group of outsiders overcome incredible adversity and long odds to find their happily-ever-after. Such themes are common in the young-adult genre, and following Harry and cheering him along gives us the escape from the mundane that fiction provides. Rowling herself is the ultimate underdog: Her rags-to-riches story defies the odds. We can't overlook this component of her books' popularity.

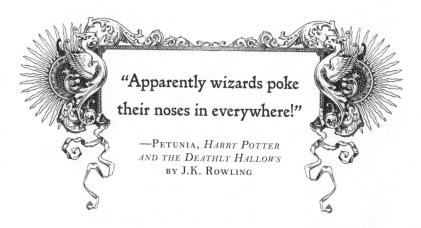

"Apparently wizards poke their noses in everywhere!"

—Petunia, *Harry Potter and the Deathly Hallows* by J.K. Rowling

Although a fairly standard fantasy plot device, Rowling's clear distinction between light and dark delivers a compelling message. We see this in the juxtaposition of Harry and Voldemort, where Voldemort represents the lust for power and Harry represents the love of brotherhood. For Rowling, love is one of, if not *the*, most powerful forces in the world. Indeed, she presents love as the most mysterious and elusive branch of magic. It was through love that Lily Potter was able to sacrifice her life and save her son from death. Voldemort, having never experienced love, continually underestimates its influence. He cannot see that love—such as the love Snape harbors for Harry's mother—could be stronger than any promise of power. As readers, we are attracted to such notions because they present a world less complicated than our own. Rowling's message that love conquers all is a compelling one.

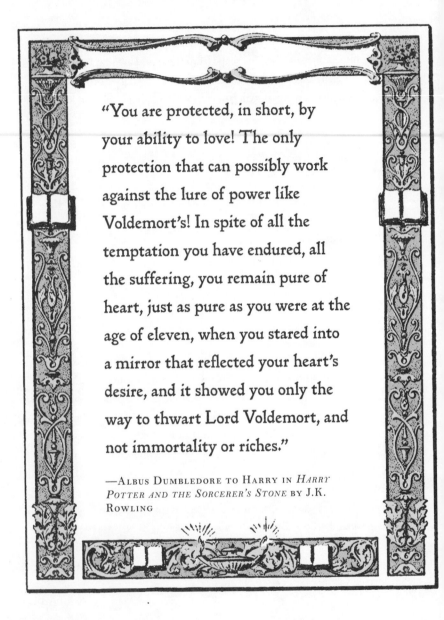

"You are protected, in short, by your ability to love! The only protection that can possibly work against the lure of power like Voldemort's! In spite of all the temptation you have endured, all the suffering, you remain pure of heart, just as pure as you were at the age of eleven, when you stared into a mirror that reflected your heart's desire, and it showed you only the way to thwart Lord Voldemort, and not immortality or riches."

—ALBUS DUMBLEDORE TO HARRY IN *HARRY POTTER AND THE SORCERER'S STONE* BY J.K. ROWLING

THE WIZARDS OF HARRY POTTER

Given the breadth of wizardry covered in this book, where can we place the wizards of Harry Potter? They do have the look of wizards, but they are also grounded in the everyday more so than Merlin, Gandalf, or a typical high-fantasy wizard. Their conjuration is a bit silly at times, and more often pedestrian than awe-inspiring. Yet, it's impossible to deny Rowling's wizards a place in the grand wizarding canon. Harry and his world are unique among wizards because of the blend of many tenets of the wizarding tradition. The magus, the sorcerer, the witch, the shaman all have seats in Hogwarts's great hall. It may be just a sketch of wizardry at times, but it still makes a compelling picture.

Rowling colors it all with her own inventions, magical and otherwise, and she injects the history of her wizards with archetypal themes of human struggle and triumph. Harry's world shares the same roots as our own and feels so close, maybe you can find it if you try; such is the great conceit of fantasy literature. It is very easy to argue that J.K. Rowling has penned a large entry in the catalogue of wizardry.

With films and worldwide translation, the Potter books easily rise to the level of a pop-culture phenomenon. No other story about wizards has generated such a volume of media, ancillary and otherwise. The Potter faithful are legion, and the series came to be synonymous with wizardry for a generation. Ultimately, the focus is less on magic and more on the story of the Boy Who Lived, but our perception of wizardry will no doubt be seen though a pair of round spectacles for the foreseeable future.

CHAPTER 8

Wizards on the Bookshelf

"He's Gandalf on crack and an IV of Red Bull, with a big leather coat and a .44 revolver in his pocket."

—AUTHOR JIM BUTCHER SPEAKING ABOUT HIS CHARACTER HARRY DRESDEN

 izards have become such a staple of the fantasy world that there is hardly a fantasy novel in print that doesn't feature one somewhere or other. For example:

- Ged in *A Wizard of Earthsea* by Ursula K. Le Guin
- Rincewind in the Discworld series by Terry Pratchett
- Jadis in *The Magician's Nephew* and Coriakin in *The Voyage of the Dawn Treader* by C.S. Lewis
- The Deryni in the Deryni series by Katherine Kurtz
- Raederle in the Riddlemaster series by Patricia McKillip
- Allanon in the Shannara series by Terry Brooks
- Raistlin Majere in the Dragonlance series by Margaret Weis and Tracy Hickman
- Various unnamed magicians in the Bartimaeus trilogy by Jonathan Stroud
- Jonathan Strange and Mr Norrell in *Jonathan Strange and Mr Norrell* by Susanna Clarke
- Merlin in *The Crystal Cave, The Hollow Hills*, and *The Last Enchantment* by Mary Stewart
- Gandalf and Saruman in *The Lord of the Rings* and *The Hobbit* by J.R.R. Tolkien

That's a lot of magic and wizardry.

 ## TOLKIEN AND THE FOUNDATIONS OF FANTASY

It's usually said that fantasy fiction begins with the publication of J.R.R. Tolkien's *The Hobbit* in 1937. This is not entirely true; a rich vein of fantasy novels dates back in some cases to the late nineteenth century. For instance, the great designer and craftsman William Morris found time to write a series of medieval fantasy romances, including *The Well at the World's End* and *The Wood Beyond the World*.

Ballantine Adult Fantasy

In 1969, Ballantine Books, then an independent publisher but now part of Random House, began publishing a series of classic fantasy novels. Edited by Betty Ballantine and with introductions by Lin Carter, the series eventually included sixty-five novels, though others published by Ballantine before the formal launch of the series are also considered part of it. The series brought attention to such classics as William Morris's medieval romances, the Kai Lung novels of Ernest Bramah, and the fantasy works of Lord Dunsany. The series ceased publication in 1974.

However, Tolkien's book ignited much of the modern passion for stories of the strange, the unearthly, and the fantastic. Above all, Tolkien introduced the archetypal wizard, Gandalf the Grey.

Gandalf in *The Hobbit*

Because Tolkien wrote *The Hobbit* to be a children's book, its treatment of Gandalf is necessarily more lighthearted than in *The Lord of the Rings*. *The Hobbit* makes a few brief references to matters outside the scope of Bilbo's quest to the Lonely Mountain and Gandalf's part in those affairs; we learn, for example, at the end of the book that Gandalf has been to a gathering of wizards and the magic users have put forth their power to drive the evil Necromancer from his stronghold in Mirkwood. In *The Lord of the Rings*, we find out that the gathering was a meeting of the White Council (which included more than just wizards), that the Necromancer was Sauron in disguise, and that after leaving his fortress of Dol Guldur in Mirkwood, he reestablished himself in Mordor. But these are matters for the future.

" 'Good Morning!' said Bilbo, and he meant it. The sun was shining, and the grass was very green. But Gandalf looked at him from under long bushy eyebrows that stuck out further than the brim of his shady hat.

'What do you mean?' he said. 'Do you wish me a good morning, or mean that it is a good morning whether I want it or not; or that you feel good this morning; or that it is a morning to be good on?' "

—J.R.R. Tolkien, *The Hobbit*

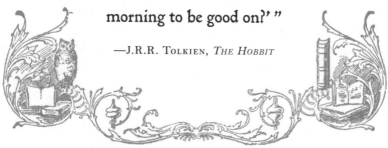

Gandalf in *The Hobbit* is an old man clad in gray with a broad-brimmed, pointed hat and bushy eyebrows and a quick temper. He, along with Thorin Oakenshield, is the chief organizer of the group of thirteen dwarves traveling to the Lonely Mountain to reclaim their lost treasure. He smokes a pipe—indeed among his magical abilities is the power to blow magic smoke rings. His other powers include calling up lightning (with which he fries a couple goblins that have attacked the party), creating light, and imitating voices (an ability he uses to good effect when the dwarves are threatened by trolls). But there is little mysterious about him.

Mithrandir

Gandalf's role is considerably expanded in *The Lord of the Rings*. Indeed, he becomes the chief Enemy of Sauron and the organizer and motivator of the forces of good during the War of the Ring. He is the counselor of kings and the confidant of elves. The hobbits Frodo and Sam, who have known him in much the same way as Bilbo Baggins of *The Hobbit*, merely as an old man with a talent for making fireworks, are constantly surprised at this new incarnation.

He goes by many names; among the elves he is called Mithrandir. He has walked Middle-earth for countless centuries, and the events of the Ring are the purpose for which he was called there. When the War of the Ring is over and a new king has been installed in Gondor, Gandalf's work is done. He takes a ship into the Undying West, along with Frodo, Bilbo, and the elves.

Yet he's not a flawless character. He can be arrogant, neglectful in telling others of his plans, solitary, and quick to anger, especially at intelligences less agile than his. Although he is the person who comes up with the plan to send the Ring in the possession of Frodo into Mordor to be destroyed, he has no way to know if this will be successful, and he is afraid when he thinks Frodo has been captured by the Enemy. Part of his attraction for us as readers is that despite his age and his exceptional powers and abilities, we can still find weaknesses with which to sympathize.

QUEEN JADIS AND CORIAKIN

Tolkien's contemporary and friend C.S. Lewis wrote his own fantasy stories—a "space" trilogy and the Narnia books, of which there are seven. Like *The Hobbit*, these books are aimed at children, but there the similarity ends. Lewis intended the books to be read as Christian allegory, so the characters within them have extremely specific roles to play.

There are two magic-wielding characters in the books (unless we count Aslan, the Christ figure, but Lewis always makes clear that his magic is exceptional and not really exactly magic): Coriakin the magician, whom Lucy Pevensie meets in *The Voyage of the Dawn Treader*, and Jadis, the White Witch, who appears in *The Magician's Nephew* and *The Lion, the Witch, and the Wardrobe*.

The Eternal Evil

In *The Lion, the Witch, and the Wardrobe*, the White Witch is killed by Aslan at the climax of the battle between her forces and those led by the Pevensies. However, in *Prince Caspian*, set several thousand years later, it's implied that she may not be dead. An evil hag implies that the witch may come back to Narnia.

"The witch!" cries Caspian. "But she's dead!"

"Oh, *is* she?" answers the hag.

Evil, Lewis seems to imply, never really dies.

Jadis

Jadis begins as the queen of another world. Only when a magical war between her and her sister devastates that world, leaving her the sole survivor, does she manage to find her way to Narnia, which Aslan has just created. There, confronted by the power of Aslan's magic, she remains a shadow of evil until at last she succeeds in taking over the land. (How she accomplishes this and how long it takes her, Lewis never explains.) As the White Witch, she casts an enchantment on Narnia, turning it to a land of ice and snow, where it is "always winter and never Christmas" as one character laments.

"Even I never dreamed of Magic like this!"

—Jadis, *The Magician's Nephew* by C.S. Lewis

Like many wizards and magic users, Jadis's weakness is her arrogance. Although she knows the danger the Pevensie children represent, she doesn't act against them until it's too late. She appeals to a magical covenant to trap Aslan and lure him to his death, forgetting the "deep magic" through which he returns from death and ultimately defeats her.

Coriakin

In contrast to Jadis, Coriakin is kindness itself, although Lucy is initially frightened of his house before he appears in it. He fits the traditional image of a wizard—tall, clad in robes, and with a trailing white beard. His spellbook is filled with such enchantments as a spell to make the speaker beautiful beyond measure; a spell that allows the caster to learn how others really feel about her; and (the spell Lucy has been charged with finding) an enchantment to make invisible things visible.

Later the reader learns that Coriakin is not, in fact, a traditional wizard. Rather, in a former existence he was a star; however, he committed some fault—just what is not specified—and was taken from the skies and set to rule a tiny island filled with foolish folk, on whom he uses his magic to maintain order.

GED OF EARTHSEA

In 1968, Ursula K. Le Guin published *A Wizard of Earthsea*. She followed it up with *The Tombs of Atuan* (1971), *The Farthest Shore* (1972), *Tehanu* (1990), and *The Other Wind* (2001). These books, in addition to some short stories set in the world of Earthsea, follow the progress of Ged, a young wizard. The books (particularly the first one) were extremely influential; a reader can see clear parallels in the development of Ged from a simple shepherd boy to a wizard to David Eddings's hero Garion, who becomes Belgarion, King of Riva and Overlord of the West, as the series progresses.

Ged, like most young boys, is impatient and wants to break through the restraints his tutor, Ogion the Silent, has placed on him. His ambition and arrogance lead him to endanger both himself and his master, who finally sends him away to a school of wizards where he can be trained properly. There, too, though Ged's ability marks him as among the first rank of pupils, his willful pigheadedness leads him to commit dangerous acts, culminating in a spell, cast during a combat with a rival student, that accidentally releases a dark and sinister spirit into the world. Much of the rest of the novel is concerned with Ged's efforts to hunt down and destroy this spirit before it does more damage to his world.

"He was fifteen, very young to learn any of the High Arts of wizard or mage, those who carry the staff; but he was so quick to learn all the arts of illusion that the Master Changer, himself a young man, soon began to teach him apart from the others, and to tell him about the true Spells of Shaping."

—URSULA K. LE GUIN, *A WIZARD OF EARTHSEA*

Among the most important lessons that Ged learns during his long apprenticeship is that although wizards can create an illusion that makes others think a person or object has changed into something else, such change remains no more than a mirage. For *true* change, to actually change one thing into another, the wizard must know its true name.

Star Wizards

Many people have argued that George Lucas's *Star Wars* series is really fantasy rather than science fiction. Seen from this point of view, the Force is magic, and the Jedi are sorcerers, using the Force to weave their spells. There's some evidence for this in the films; in *A New Hope*, an officer aboard the Death Star snaps at Darth Vader, "Don't frighten us with your sorcerer's ways, Lord Vader!"

Like Ged and Garion, Luke Skywalker is impatient and undisciplined in his use of the Force. Eventually, it takes the Jedi master Yoda—as well as a confrontation with Darth Vader—to knock some sense into him.

As in many stories, *A Wizard of Earthsea* is a story of self-discovery. Ged must pursue the shadow his uncontrolled spell released. But only by uniting with the shadow, Ged's own death, can Ged become whole and restore balance to the world.

THE MAGICIANS

In 2009, Lev Grossman made a considerable splash with his novel *The Magicians*. Critics greeted it as "Harry Potter with sex and violence." It's certainly true that the story Grossman tells has many resemblances, at least superficially, to the Potter universe. Quentin Coldwater, a smart but dissatisfied and alienated teenager, is spirited away from New York City to a secret magic school in upstate New York. The school, called Breakbills, in some respects resembles Rowling's Hogwarts: It's separated into houses (though there isn't quite the house rivalry that Rowling writes about); the classes are difficult; and students' magic abilities are, to some degree, inherited.

"Magic is really only the utilization of the entire spectrum of the senses. The humani have cut themselves off from their senses. Now they see only in a tiny portion of the visible spectrum, hear only the loudest of sounds, their sense of smell is shockingly poor and they can only distinguish the sweetest and sourest of tastes."

—HEKATE, *THE ALCHEMYST* BY MICHAEL SCOTT

However—and this is a very significant difference—according to Grossman, learning magic is both hard and boring. At one point, Quentin and a group of fellow students are sent to Antarctica for months to learn spells. The process is described as repetitive and mind-numbing. There's none of the joy in becoming a wizard that we find in other novels. Magic, in Grossman's story, is a technology to be mastered with as much effort as learning to program a computer or electrically wire a house.

Grossman borrowed from several sources, including Rowling and C.S. Lewis's Narnia stories (a series of Narnia-like stories that Quentin read as a child form an important plot point in the novel). He continued Quentin's story in *The Magician King* and *The Magician's Land*.

The wizards of Grossman's novels cast their spells largely through an intricate ritual involving extremely precise gestures. Quentin remarks several times after he enters Brakebills that the students and professors are able to move their fingers in ways he hadn't thought possible. They eschew wands (none of the Harry Potter "the wand chooses the wizard" business for them!) and generally don't speak spells very much. Spells themselves can get out of hand if not watched carefully.

As one of his school assignments, Quentin is assigned to run from Brakebills South, located in Antarctica, to the South Pole, a distance of about 300 miles. His only protection will be whatever spells he can craft to keep himself from freezing to death. He weaves a complex web of enchantments and starts running south (guiding himself by magic). After three days of ceaseless running, he begins to realize that he's starving to death because his body—covered by spells—has no way of knowing it's hungry.

 ## BELGARATH AND POLGARA

In 1982, David Eddings published *Pawn of Prophecy*. This was the first volume of a five-book series, The Belgariad. Several years after completing it, he began a second series of five books, following the same characters: The Mallorean.

The books in the two series are:

The Belgariad

- *Pawn of Prophecy*
- *Queen of Sorcery*
- *Magician's Gambit*
- *Castle of Wizardry*
- *Enchanters' End Game*

The Mallorean

- *Guardians of the West*
- *King of the Murgos*
- *Demon Lord of Karanda*
- *Sorceress of Darshiva*
- *Seeress of Kell*

The story concerns a young prince, Garion, who has been hidden away until the time is ripe for him to assume his rightful place as the Rivan King and ruler of the West. His greatest enemy is not a wizard (which would have been bad enough; there are, in fact, evil wizards who are trying to harm him) but the mad god Torak. Throughout the five books of The Belgariad, we slowly build to the climax of the meeting of Garion and Torak, a meeting from which only one can return.

At the heart of the story is the sorcerer Belgarath and his daughter Polgara. Both are extremely old; Belgarath is more than 7,000 years old and Polgara is about 3,000 years old, although she looks young (about thirty-five or so) and is extremely beautiful. Belgarath appears as an old man but doesn't seem to age beyond his current appearance. Polgara, assuming the guise of a simple farmwoman, has raised Garion from infancy. Belgarath appears at the farm from time to time during Garion's childhood, always in the guise of an elderly and dissolute man. He steals food shamelessly, often drinks too much, is normally unshaven, and in short looks as little like a 7,000-year-old wizard as is possible.

Finally, as the story progresses, he and Polgara are revealed in their true characters, and the reader learns that they are known to virtually every ruler in both the West and the East, although many think them nothing more than a myth.

Following the completion of the Mallorean, Eddings wrote two more books set in this world: *Belgarath the Sorceror* and *Polgara the Sorceress.*

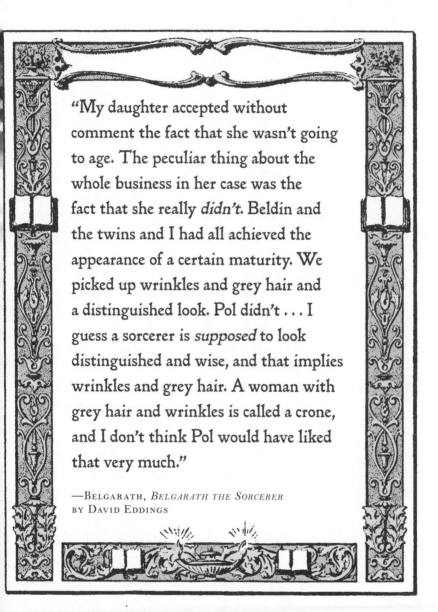

"My daughter accepted without comment the fact that she wasn't going to age. The peculiar thing about the whole business in her case was the fact that she really *didn't*. Beldin and the twins and I had all achieved the appearance of a certain maturity. We picked up wrinkles and grey hair and a distinguished look. Pol didn't . . . I guess a sorcerer is *supposed* to look distinguished and wise, and that implies wrinkles and grey hair. A woman with grey hair and wrinkles is called a crone, and I don't think Pol would have liked that very much."

—BELGARATH, *BELGARATH THE SORCERER* BY DAVID EDDINGS

HARRY DRESDEN

Not surprisingly, most wizards inhabit worlds that are unabashedly medieval. Even Harry Potter's wizarding world, although contemporary with present-day Great Britain, ignores such things as computers, e-mail, smartphones, and the rest of our ever-evolving technology. Students write their notes with quill pens at Hogwarts—not necessarily because quill pens are superior to modern ballpoints, but because medieval writing instruments seem to be more appropriate to magic.

An exception is Harry Blackstone Copperfield Dresden, hero of Jim Butcher's series of novels The Dresden Files. To date, there are fourteen novels in the series.

Harry works in Chicago, where he's a licensed private investigator and, as he tells the reader, the only wizard listed in the telephone directory.

What's in a Name?

Harry Dresden's middle names are those of two prominent stage magicians: David Copperfield (1956–) and Harry Blackstone. Actually, there were two Harry Blackstones, father and son: Harry Blackstone Sr. (1885–1965) and Harry Blackstone Jr. (1934–1997).

In the initial books of the series, Harry has relatively little contact with other wizards, although he's aware of their existence. In later books (particularly *White Nights*), he becomes obsessed with his magical heritage. His mother, Margaret Gwendolyn LeFay, was a magic user, and he has a half-brother who's also involved in the magical world.

Butcher's great strength in these books is making what Harry does seem perfectly normal in the noir world he inhabits. Harry works closely with the police, although they're highly suspicious of him.

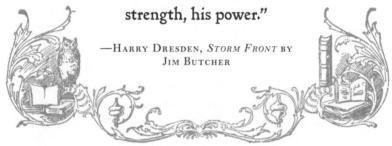

> **"A man's magic demonstrates what sort of person he is, what is held most deeply inside of him. There is no truer gauge of a man's character than the way in which he employs his strength, his power."**
>
> —HARRY DRESDEN, *STORM FRONT* BY JIM BUTCHER

As the series has continued, readers have learned more about the complex politics of the wizarding world Dresden inhabits. Dresden is a Warden of the White Council, a group of wizards whose task it is to maintain a balance and to prevent wizards from misusing their magic—though that seems to happen with some regularity. In addition, vampires have their own organizations, the Red or White Courts, and fairies owe allegiance to the Summer or Winter Courts. Later in the series, Dresden has come to suspect the existence of a Black Council, a rival to the White Council of the wizards.

Dresden, and all who are aligned with the White Council, follows the Seven Laws of Magic. These are:

1. It is prohibited to kill humans with magic.
2. It is forbidden to shapeshift others.
3. It is not allowed to probe or alter someone else's mind by means of magic.
4. It is prohibited to dominate someone else's mind.
5. It is not allowed for wizards to research or practice necromancy.
6. It is unlawful to tamper with time.
7. It is forbidden to deal with anyone or anything from another universe.

The one exception to these laws is the position of Blackstaff, a person appointed by the Council who has the right to ignore the Seven Laws and the will of the Council itself in order to preserve magical order.

As is only natural in these circumstances, Harry feels often that he can't trust any of his fellow magicians and turns for assistance instead on many occasions to Karrin Murphy, a member of the Chicago Police Department's Special Investigations unit (Special Investigations looks into cases involving the paranormal, which judging from Butcher's books constitute a good chunk of the misdeeds occurring in the Windy City).

In many respects, though, like all good noir detectives, Harry is a loner, someone fighting the amassed forces of injustice while dealing with corruption and betrayal from those allegedly on his side. In this respect, he calls up memories of the great hard-boiled detectives of 1940s fiction: Raymond Chandler's Philip Marlowe and Dashiell Hammett's Sam Spade and Ned Beaumont.

Although many wizards (including most of the ones we've been discussing) are forces for good, some are not.

PRIDE GOES BEFORE A FALL

A common theme in many stories featuring wizards is the notion of hubris, overweening pride, which inevitably leads to hubris in the form of a disaster for the wizard. This is especially true when the wizard has a seed—sometimes a bit more than a seed—of evil within him from the start.

One instance is found in the American author Clark Ashton Smith's short story "The Dark Eidolon." The beggar boy Narthos, dwelling in the city of Ummaos on the continent of Zothique, is trampled by a spirited pony ridden by the cruel prince Zotulla. Injured, Narthos drags himself out of the city and is at last rescued by a wizard living as a hermit. The old wizard teaches the boy his magical craft, and Narthos, holding his hatred of Zotulla close to him, stores up all his master's secrets.

In the years that follow, Zotulla rises to the rule of Ummaos by murdering his father. He becomes a degenerate, keeping a harem and living for pleasure alone. One day he awakens to discover that in the night a great palace has been built next to his and he learns that the great magician Namirrha has come to dwell next to the king.

Zotulla and his followers are summoned to a banquet in the palace of their new neighbor. But once there, they are seized, bound, and subjected to horrible tortures.

And here is where pride comes into things. Namirrha is, of course, none other than the poor boy Narthos, a master of wizardry now, bent on seeking revenge. But now the god Thasaidon, Lord of Evil, intervenes:

"I have helped you heretofore in all things . . . But, verily, I will not aid you in this vengeance you have planned: for the emperor Zotulla has done me no wrong and has served me well though unwittingly; and the people of Xylac, by reason of their turpitudes, are not the least of my terrestrial worshippers. Therefore, Namirrha, it were well for you to live in peace with Zotulla, and well to forget this olden wrong that was done to the beggar-boy Narthos."

Alas, Namirrha, maddened by his thirst for vengeance, refuses to obey the god. At the very moment of his triumph, when the spirit of Zotulla has been imprisoned by him in an armored and mace-wielding statue of Thasaidon, the god allows the king one moment of freedom, and lifting his weapon, Zotulla strikes down the mad wizard before death overtakes him.

Other authors chronicled similar stories of proud wizards overstepping their bounds and finding their ambitions crushed—Ged, for example, in Le Guin's *A Wizard of Earthsea*, is almost destroyed by a spirit that he lets loose while trying to cast a spell beyond his powers.

THE LOVECRAFT WIZARDS

Clark Ashton Smith was one of a number of American writers who formed a close group around the horror and fantasy writer H.P. Lovecraft. This included August Derleth, Robert E. Howard (creator of Conan the Barbarian), Frank Belknap Long, and others. Lovecraft himself created several notable evil wizards, particularly Joseph Curwen, featured in *The Case of Charles Dexter Ward*.

The novel, one of the few Lovecraft authored (he was primarily a short story writer), is set in early twentieth-century Providence, Rhode

Island, although there are several early chapters that take place in the eighteenth-century city, when Joseph Curwen was flourishing. Having arrived in Providence in 1692 (significantly, the year of the Salem witch panic in neighboring Massachusetts) as a man apparently about thirty years old, Curwen began to strike townspeople as peculiar when he apparently did not age. He maintained a business as a merchant, but his real business was bound up with his laboratory, filled with alchemical apparatuses, and his library "equipped with a remarkable battery of philosophical, mathematical, and scientific works including Paracelsus, Agricola, Van Helmont, Sylvius, Glauber, Boyle, Boerhaave, Becher, and Stahl."

Townspeople, too, remarked on the surprisingly large amounts of food that seemed to disappear into a house containing only one gentleman and a few servants. They noted that sailors on shore leave often disappeared after they were seen talking to Curwen. As the stories and rumors mounted, so did the atmosphere of vague horror that surrounded the old man.

Finally, in 1770, when Curwen must have been well over a century old but had aged no more than five years since his arrival in Providence, leading citizens gathered in secret to deal with the menace. A raiding party was organized and attacked the farm in Pawtuxet where Curwen kept his laboratory and other, less savory buildings. No one who took part in the raid would even speak of it again, but their clothing contained foul odors and their faces and hair were strangely scorched. Nearby neighbors heard shrieks and gunshots, mingled with a great light that shot up into the sky. When at last the raid was over, the old wizard was dead.

Or so they thought.

As mentioned earlier, the bulk of the novel deals with Curwen's descendant, Charles Dexter Ward, who accidentally awakens the spirit of his ancestor, still bent on fulfilling his diabolical plan to capture all wisdom from the great men and women of the past in pursuit of the ultimate power in the universe. When at last Curwen is vanquished by Ward's family doctor, Marinus Willett, it is by magic as well:

> "Even as the dogs in the yard outside began to howl, and even as a chill wind sprang suddenly up from the bay, the doctor commenced the solemn and measured intonation of that which he had meant all along to recite. An eye for an eye—magic for magic—let the outcome shew how well the lesson of the abyss had been learned! So in a clear voice Marinus Bicknell Willett began the *second* of that pair of formulae whose first had raised the writer of those minuscules— the cryptic invocation whose heading was the Dragon's Tail, sign of the *descending node*—"

The spell is successful, and the old wizard now lies scattered on the floor as a coating of bluish-green dust.

RAISTLIN MAJERE

One more well-known wizard of literature exists on the frontier between light and dark: Raistlin Majere of the Dragonlance saga.

Dragonlance was created by a talented group of artists, game designers, and writers at the company TSR, makers of Dungeons & Dragons, between 1982 and 1984. Searching for a new setting for the game, the company decided to take the then-unusual step of publishing roleplaying modules, board games, miniatures, and novels that would all reflect a world in which humans, elves, dwarves, and others struggled against the threat posed by evil dragons. Designer Tracy Hickman and editor Margaret Weis wrote the first trilogy in the series, Dragonlance Chronicles (*Dragons of Autumn Twilight*, *Dragons of Winter Night*, and *Dragons of Spring Dawning*), the first of which was published in 1984.

Among the reasons for the novels' immediate popularity was the figure of the mysterious and twisted wizard Raistlin Majere. Although Dragonlance was very much a joint effort, the figure of Raistlin has always been most associated with Weis, who, in addition to her collaborations with Hickman on other Dragonlance novels, wrote *The Soulforge* and *Brothers in Arms* (with Don Perrin), which deal exclusively with Raistlin and his brother, Caramon.

The Test of Sorcery

In the world of Dragonlance, magic is learned rather than innate (although there is a genetic predisposition toward magic). Raistlin inherited his mother's unformed magical abilities and dedicated himself to the occult arts. Always of weak health, he emerged from the arduous Test of Sorcery successful but with golden skin and hourglass eyes, seeing through them the decay of everything around him. He was also, at this point, among the most powerful sorcerers in Krynn, the world in which the Dragonlance tales are set.

Raistlin and Dungeons & Dragons

A widespread rumor exists to the effect that Raistlin and the other major characters of the Dragonlance saga, as well as the events of the saga itself, were first created by Weis and Hickman during sessions of D&D. Both authors have strenuously denied this over the years and have stated that the characters and their story emerged from their collaboration and discussions together in writing the novels.

Unlike the other heroes of the books, who are motivated by loyalty to one another and a desire to defeat the dragon overlords and bring peace to Krynn, Raistlin is driven almost entirely by self-interest.

During the course of the three novels dealing with the War of the Lance, Raistlin acquires an ancient spellbook that once belonged to the evil mage Fistandantilus. Unknown to his other companions, Raistlin has made a bargain with Fistandantilus whereby he will obtain the book in return for lending the wizard some of his life force. This ultimately impels Raistlin to turn from his original alignment, Neutral (signified by the red robes he wears), to Evil (characterized by black robes).

Raistlin's popularity among fans was such that Weis and Hickman continued his story in their next trilogy, Dragonlance Legends (*Time of the Twins*, *War of the Twins*, and *Test of the Twins*). This trilogy, largely set in Krynn's distant past, where Raistlin and several other characters have time traveled, is concerned with the mage's attempt to become a god. His failure in this attempt results in him being trapped in the Abyss and finally falling into a dreamless sleep.

For the twenty-five years in which Dragonlance novels were published, Raistlin continued to outshine all the other characters in popularity among fans. Margaret Weis has told stories of fans writing her to tell her they named their child Raistlin (a somewhat disturbing outcome, given the character's nature).

The printed stories of wizards and their deeds, both good and evil, are almost without number. But now we'll turn to their portrayal in the movies and on television in the twentieth and twenty-first centuries.

CHAPTER 9

Wizards on the Big and Small Screens

"Fantasy is an exercise bicycle for the mind. It might not take you anywhere, but it tones up the muscles that can."

—TERRY PRATCHETT

he biggest challenge filmmakers and television producers have had to overcome when they've turned their hands to fantasy and magic as subject matter is making movies and TV shows that don't look hopelessly cheesy. This was enormously difficult before the 1970s, because special effects were limited, though they could be used to great effect (for instance, in the stop-motion Ray Harryhausen films about the adventures of Hercules and Jason).

The advent of modern special effects technology, demonstrated in such films as *Star Wars: A New Hope* (1977) and mastered by George Lucas's Industrial Light and Magic company, meant that it was increasingly possible for moviemakers to create on-screen experiences that really resonated with fans of fantasy. Fans were generally thrilled by the trolls and ents in Peter Jackson's Lord of the Rings trilogy, and especially by the motion-capture technology that made possible the character of Gollum, an entirely CGI creation.

To appreciate how far we've come, it's necessary to go back to the early days of filmmaking.

THE BEGINNING

Moviemaking in the early days of Talkies was a difficult business. Sound technology was primitive, cameras were unreliable, it was nearly impossible to cut from one camera to another (if a director wanted several different angle shots, he had to have cameras running from each angle simultaneously and splice the film together in the editing room). Nonetheless, directors almost immediately wanted to tell stories of myth and magic.

In 1932, Fox Film Corporation released *Chandu the Magician*. As played by Edmund Lowe, Frank Chandler is a secret agent of the government, charged with fighting against the "secret Evil" that threatens the world. Fortunately, he's studied with yogis in the East, from whom he's learned not only yoga but also teleportation and astral projection. Armed with these magical powers, he confronts the heavy, Roxor (played by Bela Lugosi, who the previous year had first donned the black satin cape as Dracula), who has gotten hold of a death ray with which he intends to conquer the world. Chandu uses his abilities, including his mermerizing power, to thwart Roxor and destroy the death ray.

Fox followed this up two years later with *The Return of Chandu* (also titled *Chandu on the Magic Island*), which saw the magician battling an evil black magic cult. In this film, Chandu's powers have expanded a bit: He now owns a crystal ball in which he can scry things far away. He also possesses the power to make himself invisible.

The Magician

An even earlier film featuring a wizard was Rex Ingram's *The Magician*, released in 1926 and roughly based on a novel by W. Somerset Maugham. It concerns the efforts of a wizard, Oliver Haddo, to create life using the heart's blood of a virgin. Like Chandu, Haddo is skilled in hypnotism and succeeds in luring an innocent maiden (engaged to marry the hero, a brilliant heart surgeon) to his home. There he spirits her off to his laboratory, where she is—of course—rescued in the nick of time. The film appears as an odd combination of magical fantasy and mad-scientist-operating-on-beautiful-woman.

SWORDS OF THE SIXTIES

Fantasy movies were thin on the ground during the 1940s and 1950s, but the genre began to emerge in the 1960s. In 1962, United Artists released *The Magic Sword*, starring Gary Lockwood, Estelle Winwood, and Basil Rathbone as the evil wizard Lodac. When the wizard kidnaps the hero's girlfriend, the young man, George, must battle seven curses to rescue her, aided by magical armor and a sword and shield. In the end he is victorious, not only by virtue of his magical sword but with the help of his mother, a sorceress.

The Sword in the Stone

The following year saw the release of Disney's *The Sword in the Stone*, based on the first part of T.H. White's *The Once and Future King*, the story of King Arthur and Merlin. The film was voiced by a cast of relative unknowns (the voice of Merlin was Karl Swenson, later known as Lars Hanson in television's *Little House on the Prairie*). For the most part, the movie followed the book closely, ending at the point when Arthur draws the sword from the stone and is acclaimed king of England. Merlin is presented as a fussy, irritable, slightly eccentric, and ultimately loveable old magician, accompanied by his pet owl Archimedes.

The image was in stark contrast to that of the wizard in "The Sorcerer's Apprentice" section of Disney's 1940 film release, *Fantasia*. There the magician, tall with thick eyebrows and a piercing stare, is intimidating, even frightening. Merlin came as a pleasant contrast.

 WIZARDS

For the most part, Disney's treatment of wizards was relatively light—even Mickey's master in *Fantasia* won't really hurt him, he just gives Mickey a swat to remind him not to overstep his bounds again.

Such was not the case with *Wizards*, an innovative film from Ralph Bakshi, already known for pushing the limitations of animation in such socially conscious movies as *Fritz the Cat*. As in many of his films, Bakshi wanted to create a movie that was entertaining but included social commentary.

Wizards is set on a post-apocalyptic earth in which the native spirits—fairies, elves, and dwarves—who have reinhabited the land must now deal with a conflict between two wizards who are brothers and who represent the forces of good and evil. Although defeated, the evil Blackwolf retreats and finds inspiration in old films of Nazi propaganda. The ultimate aim of him and his army is to eliminate those who believe in magic over technology.

> " *Wizards* was my homage to Tolkien in the American idiom. I had read Tolkien, understood Tolkien, and wanted to do a sort of fantasy for American kids, and that was *Wizards*."

—RALPH BAKSHI

One trope featured in the film was the multiracial (i.e., fairy, elf, robot) party that seeks to destroy the evil wizard. This idea was to be repeated again and again in fantasy films, culminating in The Lord of the Rings.

Bakshi and *The Lord of the Rings*

In 1978, Bakshi released his version of The Lord of the Rings trilogy, albeit only the first half of the story. It bears similarities to Peter Jackson's later treatment of the story but it is notable mainly for its film technique, in which some sequences were shot as live-action and then traced over to create an animated effect. The film wasn't a great success and Bakshi decided not to make the second half of the story.

SWORDS AND SORCERY

Beginning in the 1980s and continuing through the next two decades, filmmakers released a stream of movies that featured bare-chested warriors, beautiful, skimpily clad maidens, and magic-brandishing wizards. The list of such films is long but includes:

- *Clash of the Titans* (1981)
- *Dragonslayer* (1981)
- *The Beastmaster* (1982)
- *Conan the Barbarian* (1982)
- *Sorceress* (1982)
- *The Sword and the Sorcerer* (1982)
- *Krull* (1983)
- *Conan the Destroyer* (1984)
- *Masters of the Universe* (1987)
- *Quest of the Delta Knights* (1993)
- *Kull the Conqueror* (1997)
- *The Scorpion King* (2002)
- *Solomon Kane* (2009)

Other movies of these years also featured wizards, but the sword and sorcery epics combined magic, violence, and sex in a way that was unique.

CONAN THE BARBARIAN

If any movie can be said to have set the standard for the sword and sorcery genre, it is John Milius's 1982 epic *Conan the Barbarian*. The film was based on the character created by the American writer Robert E. Howard. Conan appeared in a number of short stories and novels; also known as Conan of Cimmeria, he lives in the far distant past (the "Hyborian Age").

Conan's story begins with his childhood, when his village is massacred by a band of marauders led by the wizard Thulsa Doom (played by James Earl Jones). Young Conan is taken prisoner and forced into servitude. Over the years he grows in strength and determination until he "becomes" Arnold Schwarzenegger. Upon winning his freedom, he wanders Cimmeria and gathers companions with whom he wreaks vengeance on the wizard and destroys him.

"You, my children, are the water that will wash away all that has gone before. In your hand, you hold my light, the gleam in the eye of Set. This flame will burn away the darkness, burn you the way to paradise!"

—THULSA DOOM, *CONAN THE BARBARIAN*, DIRECTED BY JOHN MILIUS

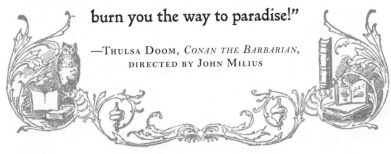

Milius appropriated Thulsa Doom for this film, although in fact the character was created by Howard as the opponent of a different character, Kull. The first story in which he appeared was written by Howard in 1928, although it was rejected, and it did not appear in print until 1967. In the story, Doom has a face "like a bare white skull, in whose eye sockets flamed livid fire." The description is interesting in light of Milius's decision to cast an African-American actor in the role.

Doom is a master of necromancy and divination, and he can also hold victims in thrall through his hypnotic powers. (Doom also appeared in comics based on Howard's works; see Chapter 10.)

MASTERS OF THE UNIVERSE

Campy as were *Conan* and its sequel, *Conan the Destroyer*, they pale in comparison to *Masters of the Universe*, based on a series of popular toys made by Mattel. The hero is actually named He-Man (played by Dolph Lundgren), and his opponent is the wizard Skeletor (Frank Langella, who must have really needed the money) and his second in command, Evil-lyn.

Skeletor is blue, and a hood covers his head, but his face is shown as a skull. The explanation given is that his flesh was burned away, leaving only the bones, which are magically protected from decay.

Cartoon Series

Skeletor, He-Man, and their companions were featured in a cartoon series that ran 1983–1985. This series established the basic backstory: that He-Man is, in fact, Prince Adam, son of King Radnor and Queen Marlena (the latter of whom is an earth woman). In the time-honored tradition of superheroes, the prince pretends to be a good-for-nothing layabout, but when he says the magic words, "By the power of Greyskull!" he is transformed into He-Man.

Plans for a second movie were made, and as of 2014 *Greyskull: Masters of the Universe* continues to undergo script revisions, with no production date set.

EXCALIBUR

Hollywood finally started to take its wizards seriously with the 1981 film *Excalibur*, directed by John Boorman. Although a number of films have been based in whole or in part on the legend of King Arthur (see Chapter 4), *Excalibur* was the first to try to encompass the entire legend more or less as it had been told in Thomas Malory's *Le Morte d'Arthur*.

In the movie, Merlin is portrayed by British actor Nicol Williamson as eccentric, frightening, powerful, and sorrowful. He is vulnerable to love (it's strongly implied in one scene that he and Morgana become lovers, the means by which he is ultimately ensnared by her magic), occasionally blind to the future, but ultimately triumphant in his vision for Arthur's kingdom.

"Look upon this moment. Savor it! Rejoice
with great gladness! Great gladness!
Remember it always, for you are joined by
it. You are One, under the stars. Remember
it well, then . . . this night, this great victory.
So that in the years ahead, you can say, 'I was
there that night, with Arthur, the King!' For
it is the doom of men that they forget."

—MERLIN, *EXCALIBUR*, DIRECTED BY JOHN BOORMAN

Boorman's main achievement in the film is to make a complex story comprehensible, albeit with a lot of very mystical scenes, and to create in Merlin a character who is odd without being silly. This Merlin, unlike Disney's earlier variant, demands to be taken seriously. In the end, after taking his revenge on Morgana (he tricks her into using the Spell of Making in such a way that it drains her of her youth and shows her as the hideous hag she has become; when she encounters her son, Mordred, he

strikes her down in horror), Merlin fades into the land of dreams and legends where, ultimately, Arthur will reside as well.

PETER JACKSON AND *THE LORD OF THE RINGS*

Of all film treatment of wizards, Peter Jackson's magnificent three-film version of J.R.R. Tolkien's *The Lord of the Rings* is by far the most impressive. Jackson followed this by releasing a three-film treatment of Tolkien's earlier work, *The Hobbit.*

The films have been widely acclaimed both by fans of the literary volumes and by people who have never read a word of Tolkien's works. Although the trilogy omitted some significant parts of the story and changed others, most who see the movies are astonished at how true to Tolkien's vision the movies have remained.

This is particularly impressive, given previous filmic treatment of Tolkien's work.

The Animated Versions

We've already mentioned Ralph Bakshi's 1978 version of the first part of Tolkien's story. In addition, two other animated attempts were made to bring the world of Middle-earth to life.

In 1977, Saul Bass Productions created a cartoon version of *The Hobbit* for television. It featured the voices of Orson Bean as Bilbo, Richard Boone as Smaug the dragon, and John Huston as Gandalf. The production was aimed at a young audience, and perhaps for that reason the producers felt compelled to put in songs (although, to be fair, Tolkien himself included a number of songs in *The Hobbit* including such classics as "The Road Goes Ever On" and "Fifteen Birds in Five Fir Trees").

Although the movie makes for painful viewing today, it found a surprisingly warm reception at the time. Huston, the famed director and actor, did a credible job of bringing gravitas to the role of Gandalf and making the wizard the core of the party of dwarves and one hobbit, traveling to the East to recover a dragon-plundered treasure.

In 1980, a second animated musical version of Tolkien was released: *The Return of the King*. John Huston reprised his role as Gandalf, as did Bean the role of Bilbo (he also added the role of Frodo). Because Bakshi had no intention of returning to Tolkien, this movie has come to be regarded as a sequel to the Bakshi film. Once again, audiences were subjected to a battery of painful songs, sung in this case by Glenn Yarbrough ("the minstrel of Gondor").

Gandalf in both these movies has moments of power and authority, but for the most part he comes across as a silly old man, closer to T.H. White's Merlin than to Tolkien's conception of him.

For years, rumors circulated among Tolkien fans that there would be a live-action version of their beloved story. Then, in 1999 it was confirmed that principal photography had begun, not just on a single film of the story but on a trilogy, all of which would be filmed simultaneously.

Three films to Rule Them All

When Jackson first began contemplating making a live-action film of *The Lord of the Rings*, he and his collaborator Fran Walsh wrote a treatment for two movies: one that took the story through the events of *The Fellowship of the Ring* and *The Two Towers*, and the second that covered *The Return of the King*. In discussions with New Line Cinema (the company that wound up as Jackson's producers), an executive asked them why, given that the books were in the form of a trilogy, they didn't just make three films. Jackson and Walsh and Philippa Boyens agreed and began rewriting their scripts.

In the key role of Gandalf, Jackson cast veteran British actor Ian McKellen. Although McKellen agreed to play the part, he was conscious that it would mean an enormously busy schedule for him, as he was also playing arch-villain Magneto in Bryan Singer's trilogy of superhero films about Marvel's X-Men.

Filming of Jackson, Walsh, and Boyens's scripts took place in New Zealand and lasted for more than a year. It was the single greatest film project ever undertaken; an entire city, Minas Tirith, was built as a set, as well as the hilltop palace of Théoden, King of Rohan. There were thousands of extras, and endless hours of work on special effects, armor construction, sword-fighting training, and much more.

A Wizard Is a Wizard

Ian McKellen, of course, plays Gandalf in The Lord of the Rings films. Richard Harris originated the role of Dumbledore in the Harry Potter film franchise, a role that was taken over by Michael Gambon in 2002 after Harris's death.

"I often get mistaken for Dumbledore," McKellen observes. "One wizard is very much like another." Gambon has the same experience, and McKellen once asked him what he did when he was mistaken for McKellen by autograph hunters. "Oh," replied Gambon, "I just sign your name."

The Battle with the Balrog

Gandalf the wizard has a number of great moments throughout the films, but perhaps his most impressive is his confrontation with the balrog, the great spirit of the underworld, on the Bridge of Khazad-dûm in the mines of Moria.

At this point the Fellowship of the Ring has been defeated in its attempt to cross the Misty Mountains, making its way toward the dark land of Mordor. Spies of the evil wizard Saruman have already marked their way, and Gandalf, in a moment of desperation, determines that they should go not *over* the mountains but *under* them through the long-deserted mines of Moria.

There they find horror as they discover that a group of dwarves seeking to reoccupy the mine has been slaughtered by orcs. Shortly after, the party itself is attacked by orcs, accompanied by a cave troll. Just when they've escaped from that battle, a huge flaming monster, carrying a sword and a whip, appears, chasing them across a narrow bridge that leads toward the outside and safety.

Gandalf turns and confronts the creature, a balrog of Morgoth. "I am a servant of the secret fire!" he declares. "You shall not pass!"

The balrog raises his sword, and the wizard brings down his staff on the bridge. The slender span crumbles and falls into the abyss, taking the balrog with it, as the audience sighs in relief.

Then, from far below, the thongs of the balrog's whip swing up and catch on Gandalf's legs, dragging him to the edge. He clutches at the stone, slips, and disappears with a cry.

This moment is the emotional heart of the film. Up until now, Gandalf has been the party's leader and the prime mover in everything going forward. Now, in the early stages of the quest, he is lost. Aragorn, heir to the throne of the West, must assume the leadership and the party will have to make due without Gandalf's strength and wisdom.

Jackson's film allows us to feel the horror of the moment, combined with the urgency of the battle. The party can't stop to mourn its loss; only when they have passed through the eastern gates of Moria can they weep for their fallen companion.

Fans who were horrified at the death of the old wizard could relax after the second film, *The Two Towers*, appeared in 2002. There, Gandalf was not only resurrected as Gandalf the White, but he engaged in an epic confrontation with his enemy Saruman at the latter's tower of Orthanc. Gandalf emerged more powerful than ever and led the forces of good to their final victory in *The Return of the King*, which released in 2003.

DUNGEONS & DRAGONS

Wizards have been an essential part of the grandfather of roleplaying fantasy games since its creation in 1974 (see Chapter 10). So it's not surprising that a wizard would feature heavily in the first live-action movie based on the game. Sadly, the results were unimpressive.

Dungeons & Dragons, released in 2000, starred Jeremy Irons as the evil mage Profion, who is seeking a magic rod that will allow him to control dragons. He's thwarted in his plans by a pair of not terribly competent thieves, played by Justin Whalin and Marlon Wayans, and an apprentice mage played by Zoe McLellan. Along the way, they must battle thieves, Profion's blue-lipped henchman Damodar, a skeleton and other assorted creatures, and finally Profion himself in a climactic battle involving dozens of dragons.

Considering the widespread popularity of D&D in the 1980s and 1990s, this film should have been better than it was. Irons, who clearly never took the project seriously, chewed the scenery unmercifully, while the other actors were mostly overwhelmed by bad screenwriting and mediocre special effects.

Later D&D films

To fulfill contractual obligations to Wizards of the Coast, owners of Dungeons & Dragons, two more D&D films were made: *Wrath of the Dragon God* (2005) and *The Book of Vile Darkness* (2012). Both were direct-to-TV movies, both included wizards in their cast of characters, and both were savaged by critics. There are indications that another D&D film may be in the works, but this will depend on the outcome of legal battles between Hasbro (the parent company of Wizards of the Coast) and various other litigants.

WIZARDS ON TELEVISION

Magic on the small screen suffered from many of the same problems as in the movies: The magic spells had to look convincing, or else they just looked silly. Wizards would occasionally appear in such 1960s standards as *Bewitched*, but no one took them seriously.

By 1980, things had changed—somewhat. In the 1980–81 season, CBS ran *Mr. Merlin*, a comedy about Merlin living in the twentieth century and forced to take on an assistant. Merlin (played by Barnard Hughes) is crusty and grumpy, whereas his assistant Zac (Clark Brandon) is eager-eyed and bumbling. The sitcom had some amusing moments, but failed to find an audience.

CBS executives weren't ready to give up, and in 1983 they tried out *Wizards and Warriors* starring Jeff Conaway. Clive Revill, a veteran British stage actor, appeared as Vector, an evil wizard bent on the destruction of the hero, Prince Erik Greystone. Scripts were a mixture of drama, comedy, and deliberate camp.

Although critics praised the show as witty, viewers didn't flock to it, and it was cancelled at the end of the season.

The D&D Cartoon

In the early 1980s, Dungeons & Dragons was at the height of its popularity. Little wonder then that CBS, in 1983, launched a cartoon based on the popular roleplaying game. Unlike D&D itself, which is always set in a fictional universe, the cartoon premised that six friends, going on a D&D carnival ride, are magically transported to a world threatened by Tiamat, a five-headed dragon. They are also threatened by Venger, a powerful wizard.

Each of the friends becomes a D&D "class": ranger, cavalier, thief, magician (more a prestidigitator than a wizard, in this case), acrobat, and barbarian. Venger, their opponent, is a corrupted magic user whose spells, though not always conforming to D&D rules, are nonetheless powerful and dangerous.

Despite its campiness, the show was a hit, leading its time slot for two years. Today, it remains a sentimental favorite among many D&D fans.

BUFFY AND CHARMED

After a short hiatus, magic- and wizard-themed shows returned in the 1990s with a vengeance. The two that had the most impact were *Buffy the Vampire Slayer*, which starred Sarah Michelle Gellar and ran from 1997 to 2003 on the WB and UPN networks, and *Charmed*, which starred Shannen Doherty, Alyssa Milano, and Holly Marie Combs and lasted from 1998 to 2006 on the WB.

Buffy the Vampire Slayer

Taking off from a mildly successful 1992 film about a high school girl fighting vampires, *Buffy* the television show, under the visionary eye of Joss Whedon, became a blockbuster. Buffy Summers, the all-American high school girl, turns out to be the chosen slayer of vampires and assorted other creatures. She's backed by a trusty gang of high school nerds and oddballs, including Xander Harris, Willow Rosenberg, Cordelia Chase, and Buffy's "Watcher," Rupert Giles.

Willow begins as the brains of the group, the geeky student who does library research, hiding behind her shyness. By the end of the second season, not only had the character grown in assertiveness, she began to study magic and eventually became a full-fledged witch. Her powers grow as she becomes more adept and eventually she almost equals Buffy in destroying monsters. By the end of the series, she is arguably even more powerful than the Slayer, capable of destroying the world if she so chose.

The means by which Willow practices magic were never made entirely clear by the show's creators; she used traditional spells and elements associated with witchcraft and wizardry, and there's mention of the fact that doing magic is physically draining. Because most of the magic in the Buffyverse is performed by females, it's an interesting coincidence that Willow's power grows considerably when she becomes involved in a lesbian relationship with another character.

Charmed

The power of female magic was also much on display in *Charmed*. In this show, the lead characters are witches (although, as in Harry Potter, there's no great distinction in the show made between witches and wizards except that witches are female).

Three sisters, members of the Halliwell family, discover that they come from a long line of witches. They have in their possession a book of spells, called the Book of Shadows, which they use to battle demons, evil warlocks, and various other creatures and foes. Each sister, in addition, has her own special power (scrying, telekinesis, and "freezing" people or objects mid-motion).

Changed *Charmed*

Shannen Doherty, who played Prue Halliwell on the show, had a long history of not getting along with her fellow actors, and this proved true in *Charmed*. By 2001 things had deteriorated so much between her and Alyssa Milano, who played Phoebe, that Doherty was fired from the show and replaced with Rose McGowan. She played Paige, a hitherto unknown Halliwell sister.

Magic for the sisters is hereditary, though its specific forms are unpredictable. In the later episodes of the show, Paige became an expert at mixing potions—she got the recipes from the Book of Shadows. Much like potions concocted by other fictional witches and wizards, they often required bizarre ingredients—in fact, the more complex the spell, the weirder its material components.

THE WIZARDS OF WAVERLY PLACE

From 2007 to 2012, the Disney Channel ran *The Wizards of Waverly Place*, aimed at a young audience and starring Selena Gomez, David Henrie, and Jake T. Austin. The show told the story of three children, each having magical abilities. They live with their parents in Manhattan and, on the surface, lead ordinary lives. However, their father is a former wizard (their mother is mortal), and eventually they will have to decide who inherits the family's magical powers.

There exists, in parallel to the mortal world inhabited by the Russos—the family name is Russo—a magical world that they can visit from time to time to receive advice, instructions, and assistance. In the end, a finale titled "Who Will Be the Family Wizard?" drew 10 million viewers, who saw Selena Gomez's Alex assume the title of Russo family wizard.

Like many shows about magic and wizards, *The Wizards of Waverly Place* generated a video game. And it is to the video game industry and its ancestor, fantasy roleplaying games, that we now turn.

CHAPTER 10

Wizards in Games and Comics

n the first two decades of the twenty-first century, games and comics have become a central part of our cultural experience. We've already mentioned manga (see Chapter 6) as a significant literature in Japan that has spread to America and elsewhere. American comics as well picked up steam in the last years of the twentieth century and have continued their growth into the twenty-first.

As well, the video-gaming industry has come into its own since the turn of the century. Home gaming systems have become a common household appliance. Games are no longer the sole domain of teenage boys and no longer restricted to sticky-floored arcades. Indeed, according to the Entertainment Software Association, the average age of gamers in 2013 was thirty years; more than half of all Americans play video games and own at least one dedicated gaming console. The gender gap

is also shrinking with 45 percent of gamers being female,
and women over eighteen
representing a greater per-
centage of gamers than boys
under seventeen. Attitudes
have shifted as well: Parents
play with their children—and
are often defeated by them in
the games. The games them-
selves have evolved to com-
plexities undreamed of by the creators of the humble Pac-Man. We now
have games in the genres of action, puzzle, strategy, trivia, social media,
and more. Fantasy-based roleplaying video games provide us with
immersive worlds and fully realized characters, both in terms of story
and artistic rendering. In this world, the wizard is a persistent fixture.

DUNGEONS & DRAGONS

To fully understand the development of video games and, in particular, to understand the central role that wizards and spellcasting play in
many of them, we need to trace their history back to the most important fantasy tabletop game of all: Dungeons & Dragons.

Conceived by Gary Gygax and Dave Arneson in the 1970s, Dungeons & Dragons is a scion of the comic book era. It was an unprec-
edented hit when it was first introduced in 1974, building in the
war-gaming community and spreading to the student populations of
high schools and colleges. The initial popularity of D&D spawned
a slew of other tabletop roleplaying games, often spin-offs of other

franchises, from one-offs such as James Bond and Ghostbusters to ongoing series such as Star Trek and the DC and Marvel comic universes. In summer 2014, Wizards of the Coast, the current owner of the franchise, released a fifth edition of the core rulebooks, forty years after the game's initial publication.

Yet, perhaps surprising in today's whiz-bang world of huge special effects, bursting fireballs, and sparkling spells, D&D involves nothing more than a group of friends sitting around a table, papers and pencils spread out before them, each with a little heap of polyhedral dice, and at one end of the table, the Dungeon Master, his papers and dice concealed behind a cardboard screen, reading out the words of an adventure.

"Okay, the party is in a narrow corridor, ten feet wide. By the torchlight, you can see that up ahead it forks left and right. Which way do you want to go?"

"Uh . . . let's go left. But get a spell ready!"

"You reach the fork and turn left. Ahead is nothing but darkness. To your right, you hear a rustling."

"I look right!"

"You see, stumbling out of the darkness, a mummy, its arms reaching out to grasp you."

"Cast Magic Missile! Cast Magic Missile!"

"All right. Roll a twenty-sided die."

In the 1970s and 1980s, millions of kids were spending their afternoons this way, sitting in their parents' basement rec rooms and having adventures in fighting mummies, zombies, orcs, kobolds, and, of course, dragons.

Build Your Own Adventure

The idea for D&D grew out of war games that hobbyists such as Gygax and Arneson played with medieval-themed miniatures. But D&D

departed from previous war games in that the players controlled individual characters instead of military units. Players create "characters" or avatars, assigning them various traits such as strength, constitution, and intelligence, as well as a specialization ("lock picking," "learning languages," etc.). These characters then embark upon adventures within a fantasy setting that is either preprinted by D&D's parent company or invented by the Dungeon Master. The DM leads the meeting of the characters and presents them with challenges, referees battles with various monsters (determining the outcome by rolling various combinations of dice), and acts out player encounters with nonplayer characters. In the process the players earn experience points for their characters, which are then spent on various abilities to increase the powers of their avatars.

No One Wins, Everyone Wins

A unique aspect of D&D, and indeed any roleplaying game, is that there is no winner. Players accumulate experience points (which, in turn, enhance their abilities, on the theory that the more experience you have with something, the better you get at it) and encounter more and more challenging obstacles. The game ends only when the players tire of it; some D&D games have continued for decades.

Wizards, among the most important player "classes," choose a specialization. This allows them greater power in one magical school, but reduces their range of spells from which to choose. But it is common for a wizard to style him- or herself as not only a spellcaster but also as a philosopher, inventor, and scientist of the arcane. As we have seen in other games, wizards are a class unto themselves, contrasting with other magic-using D&D classes such as Cleric, Druid, Monk, Psion, and Sorcerer.

In the fourth edition of the game, a wizard has access to eight schools of magic, augmented by their chosen specialization:

- Abjuration: spells of protection and banishment
- Conjuration: summoning of monsters or materials
- Divination: spells that reveal information
- Enchantment: magically imbuing a character or giving the caster power over a target
- Evocation: spells that employ energy
- Illusion: altering perception
- Necromancy: spells that manipulate life force
- Transmutation: transformation of creatures or objects

A small number of spells do not fall into these schools, and are known as universal spells, which are available to all wizards. Further specialized classes of the wizard in more advanced game sets include:

- Archmage
- Cerebremancer
- Hierophant
- Loremaster
- Metamind
- Pyrokineticist
- Thaumaturgist
- Cosmic Descryer

New Editions, New Rules

Over the years, a number of new editions of D&D have been released, each altering some of the rules. Wizards have remained a player class throughout the game's history, although the specific rules governing their play have changed. In 2014, Wizards of the Coast, owner of D&D, released a new edition, the fifth in the history of the game.

The acquisition of spells and the mechanics of spellcasting for the D&D wizard are unique among game wizards. Most new spells are learned though copying magical writings into a spellbook, a method that allows wizards to master any number of permissible spells once they discover them.

Although wizards can assemble a broad and versatile arsenal of powers, they require preparation prior to spellcasting. A wizard needs comfortable quiet areas to study or meditate so the spell can be subconsciously "stored" until a trigger releases the spell's power. When he wishes to cast a spell, a wizard will often appear to be in a trance as his consciousness recalls the memory of the spell. When he finds the spell he wants, the wizard then completes the trigger sequence: voicing several strange words, utilizing some arcane component, or perhaps making a quirky hand movement. Every part of the sequence must be exact or else the wizard may miscast, misfire, cast an entirely different spell, or cast nothing at all. This is the easiest and most efficient way to cast spells because the wizard needs only to perform the trigger element of the spell when the need arises. But this presents a weakness in that wizards cannot cast spells they have not prepared, and once a spell is used it must be recommitted to memory. This is the limiting factor to a wizard's power. Wizards can develop foresight to enhance their

problem-solving abilities and anticipate which spells may be most useful in a given situation.

NOTABLE D&D WIZARDS

A Dungeon Master can invent her own adventure or crib a template
from a prewritten campaign. Campaigns are preset scenarios in imagined worlds, and D&D has supported many different campaigns over the
years. Three of the best known are the Greyhawk, Forgotten Realms,
and Dragonlance campaigns. We've already mentioned Dragonlance,
featuring Raistlin Majere, the dark and twisted wizard with the hourglass eyes (see Chapter 1); and the Forgotten Realms, in which dwell
Elminster Aumar of Shadowdale and Khelben 'Blackstaff' Arunsun (see
Chapter 1). It remains to explore one more of Dungeons & Dragons's
most famous wizards, one who inhabits its oldest world.

Mordenkainen of Greyhawk

Mordenkainen is a fictional wizard first created by Gary Gygax
as an avatar for his personal game world of Greyhawk. Mordenkainen
is therefore one of the oldest characters continuously associated with
D&D. When, in an orgy of corporate maneuvering in 1985, Gygax was
forced out of TSR, the original publisher of Dungeons & Dragons, he
lost the rights to characters he had created, including Mordenkainen.

The character was reimagined as the world's most powerful wizard,
and he has played diverse roles as both hero and villain in the expanded
Greyhawk universe; he is an important figure in the fictional history
of the Flanaess, the eastern part of the continent of Oerik, one of the
four continents of Greyhawk's fictional world of Oerth. Mordenkainen
operates under a Neutral alignment, attempting to maintain a balance

between Good and Evil. His preferred method of influence is to operate from the shadows.

He has traveled extensively in Greyhawk, possibly resided for a time in the City of Greyhawk, and gathered around him a coterie of disciples, known as the Obsidian Citadel, although it was dissolved after the Battle of Emridy Meadows.

Mordenkainen's goal is to keep peace in the land; in this respect he is similar to Elminister in the Forgotten Realms. His appearance is similar as well (both mages bear a striking resemblance, unsurprisingly, to Gandalf the Grey): He is tall, wears long boots, sports a Van Dyke beard streaked with gray, and carries a magical staff. Like Gandalf, he is impatient and says less than he knows.

The Worlds and Wizards of D&D

Greyhawk, Dragonlance, and the Forgotten Realms are not the only D&D campaign worlds. Over the game's forty-year history, many others have been developed. These include Planescape, Eberron, and Dark Sun. The Mystara campaign setting is the combined work of several semi-independent groups that were assigned the task of developing different cultures and nations for the worlds supported by D&D. Countless wizards exist on Alphatia, such as Haldemar of Haaken, Terari, and Empress Eriadna.

VIDEO GAME WIZARDS

Video games grew out of the experience of Dungeons & Dragons's tell-your-own-adventure ethos (unsurprisingly, many video game designers were and are D&D enthusiasts) combined with improving technology during the 1980s and 1990s. The wizard has been a staple class in games since the first fantasy-adventure video games were conceived.

In a fantasy video game, as in Dungeons & Dragons, a player is represented by an avatar with a certain skill specialization, commonly called his or her "class." Typically, a game wizard wields a staff or a wand. Cloth is the given armor designation—the lightest and least protective material. A wizard deals damage by targeting an enemy and casting a spell, which can take time or be instant. Longer spells usually are more powerful, and some spells require the use of a catalyst or reagent. While casting, a wizard is vulnerable to attack or interruption of the cast, which encourages the use of so-called crowd-control spells to keep enemies at range. In many games wizards use mana as a resource, which limits the number of spells they can cast consecutively. They draw power from the arcane and spells are most often broken into elemental schools. This makes them different than warlocks or necromancers who use the powers of darkness and death. Although the magical energy from which a wizard draws his powers may have different names depending on the game, the basic principle remains the same: The wizard's power is limited, not infinite, and it takes time to recharge.

Mana Points and Costs

Mana points are the method by which wizards cast their spells. Each spell has a mana cost, and the number of spells a wizard can cast is limited by the size of the caster's mana pool. A caster's mana typically regenerates over time or can be restored by consuming magic potions. The concept of mana as a magical resource arose in roleplaying games, which allegedly took their inspiration from Larry Niven's fantasy story "The Magic Goes Away."

Blowing Up Pixels

Video game wizards really came into their own with the advent of a class of game called dungeon crawlers: games with the primary goal of clearing increasingly difficult levels of monsters, traps, and puzzles, and collecting bigger and bigger treasures. Arguably the original dungeon crawler, Gauntlet (first published in 1985) allows a player to select one of four characters to do battle against hordes of swarming monsters in a series of increasingly complex mazes. Each character has his or her own unique strength: The Warrior is the strongest, the Wizard has the most powerful magic, the Valkyrie has the best armor, and the Elf moves the fastest. The Wizard's magic missile is able to take out monsters with fewer hits, but he is not terribly durable and can be easily overwhelmed if not careful. Due to its success in the arcades, Gauntlet was ported to over fourteen different home systems of the day including the original Atari and Nintendo systems.

Games such as Blizzard's Diablo franchise, now in its third install-ment, have refined the dungeon crawler into an art form. The main challenge a dungeon crawler offers is facing off against vast waves of low-health enemies, which are fairly easily dispatched, but play can quickly get out of control if players are not careful. Combat in Diablo III is about choosing your targets carefully and controlling the battlefield. The Wizard character has a large catalogue of spells to choose from to accomplish this, including Shock Pulse, Arcane Torrent, Frost Nova, Wave of Force, Energy Armor, and many more. The Diablo Wizard is a young and reckless magic-wielder, exploring dangerous arcane arts and unleashing her power to deadly blood-soaked effect on the battlefield.

The Elder Scrolls is a series of action roleplaying open-world fantasy video games known for their elaborate and richly detailed worlds. This series mixes elements of the dungeon crawler into a mostly roleplaying genre. The editions Morrowind, Oblivion, and Skyrim, have all won Game of the Year awards from multiple outlets. In Skyrim, the most recent console release, elves and half-elves are the races that begin with advantages in certain magical areas, but there are no caster classes per se, although a player can choose to join the Mage's Guild and focus his skill points in magical abilities. The recently released massive multiplayer online game Elder Scrolls Online includes a caster class in the form of the Sorcerer. This is a powerful caster class that manipulates natural forces and summons minions in addition to using dark magic to crowd-control and damage enemies. In the Elder Scrolls universe, "wizard" is a rank of spellcaster below Master Wizard and above Warlock. Ocato, Imperial Battlemage of Emperor Uriel Septim VII, and Mirabelle Ervine, Master Wizard of the College of Winterhold, are two notable mages among many nonplayer characters the gamer encounters.

Wizarding Antagonists

As in novels and comics, wizards are frequently enemies in video games. Manannan of the long-running King's Quest series is an old, evil wizard who kidnaps infant boys to serve as his slaves. He is one among many wizards in the series, but he is notable for reigning as the absolute ruler of the land of Llewdor for many years, where under his leadership brigands, thieves, and the like prosper. His final servant, the king's son, is able to escape the clutches of Manannan and turn him into a cat. King Graham later encounters Manannan and captures him in sack of peas. Manannan's namesake is a sea deity of Irish myth known as Manannán mac Lir.

The Nintendo universe offers us a wizard in Ganondorf, a classic villain and venerable end boss in the classic Legend of Zelda series. Zelda is another game that exists between a dungeon crawler and role-playing game; some considered it a spiritual forerunner of video RPGs.

From Japan to America

In 1986, when Japanese culture was being imported into America on a large scale, Nintendo released the original Legend of Zelda, which had first been developed by two Japanese designers, Shigeru Miyamoto and Takashi Tezuka. It is considered one of the most important early video games.

Ganon, as he is ultimately known, is the archenemy of the hero Link. He embarks on an evil quest to conquer the kingdom of Hyrule, and seeks godlike power to facilitate this. His specific motives vary from game to game, but most often they include capturing Princess Zelda and seeking the full Triforce, a powerful magical relic that gives him godlike strength and boundless mystical power. It also makes him invulnerable to all but the most powerful weapons, such as the Master Sword. He is a formidable sorcerer, able to use magic to attack as well as shapeshift, and he is a skilled swordsman should the need arise. Despite his size, Ganon is incredibly agile, and can dodge sword attacks and arrows. The Triforce also makes Ganon stronger, granting him powers such as teleportation and superhuman strength. He has survived injuries as severe as having an entire castle collapse on him and being impaled by a sword. Ganon can only be dealt the final blow with the Master Sword, but his followers may resurrect him should the need arise. It explains how he is able to be the villain in over fifteen editions of the Zelda franchise.

MMORPGs AND IMMERSIVE GAMEPLAY

In 1999, gamers all over America were having a completely new experience: playing Everquest, the first breakout in a new type of video game. Everquest was a massive, multiplayer, online roleplaying game (MMORPG), and the gaming landscape would never look the same again.

In Everquest, players from all over the country—all over the world—linked into a server and their avatars appeared on each other's screens. The avatars could interact, fight each other, or band together to fight monsters. It was, in short, like being in a worldwide session of Dungeons & Dragons.

Even in early online MMOs such as RuneScape and Ultima Online, which featured limited customization and character classes, magic was still a prominent component of gameplay. Everquest was one of the first widely popular MMOs and boasts four magic-using classes: wizard, magician, necromancer, and enchanter. The Harry Potter-esque Wizard 101 is in the trend of more recent free-to-play online MMOs. In this family-friendly game, all the avatars are some form of wizard and they duel other wizards or creatures to advance their level and increase character power.

Alphabet Soup

It's easy for non-initiates to get lost in the acronyms peculiar to hobby gaming. Here's a short list:

- RPG: Roleplaying Game. This can refer to tabletop games such as D&D or to video games.
- MMO: Massive Multiplayer Online. A game in which players are linked together on their computers by a server.
- FPS: First-Person Shooter. A game in which the camera angle reflects the avatar's point of view.
- TBS: Turn-Based Strategy. Players take turns.
- RTS: Real-Time Strategy. Game play happens in real time.

These acronyms can be combined. For instance, MMORTS means massive multiplayer real-time strategy game.

Final Fantasy is one of the longest running MMO series. Up to a fourteenth release, it has a complicated backstory matching the twisted connections you find in the arc of a comic book plot. The franchise centers around a series of fantasy/sci-fi RPGs, but includes motion pictures, anime, printed media, and other merchandise. The titular game in the series was published in 1987, and although most Final Fantasy installments are stand-alone stories with different settings and main characters, they feature identical elements that define the franchise.

The wizards of the Final Fantasy series are known as simply mages, often with an associated color: Black mages practice offensive magic; Blue mages copy enemy abilities; Red mages are generalists; Summoners are conjurers; Time mages manipulate time and space; White mages are healers; Green mages practice the Green magic, which enhances allies' abilities and weakens enemies. As the series progressed, "wizard" became synonymous with the Black mage. Other Final Fantasy titles merged the features of Green, Black, and White mages.

> "Can a magician kill a man by magic?"
> Lord Wellington asked Strange. Strange
> frowned. He seemed to dislike the question.
> "I suppose a magician might," he admitted,
> "but a gentleman never would."
>
> —SUSANNA CLARKE, *JONATHAN STRANGE*
> *AND MR NORRELL*

World of Warcraft

World of Warcraft is one of the most successful PC games of all time. Peaking at 13 million worldwide subscribers, WoW is the model of the MMO genre. The year 2015 marks the tenth anniversary of the WoW game, and the original Warcraft RTS games reach even deeper into history. This alone is a remarkable accomplishment in the video game industry. The mage Jaina Proudmoore, leader of the Kirin Tor, is the prototypical wizard in Warcraft lore and novelizations, having had a hand in all major events since the third installment of the

RTS series. Other wizardlike classes in WoW include the warlock, the shaman, and the shadow priest. The warlock, for example, is a spellcaster who uses fire and shadow magic against his enemies, in addition to summoned demons. Warlocks can specialize in damage-over-time spells in the Affliction specialization, burst damage in the Destruction specialization, or more powerful minions in the Demonology specialization.

The mage class fills the role of elite damage-dealer. Additionally incorporating crowd-control in the form of Polymorph and Frost Nova spells, the mage is also formidable in player-versus-player combat. Magi can summon bursts of fire to incinerate their foes, shatter bones with lances of ice, and demolish their targets with arcane missiles. Although they wield powerful offensive spells, mages are very poor at physical combat. They wear cloth armor, and they have no ability to heal themselves without the use of their potions or bandages. Mage talents focus on enhancing individual schools of magic.

WIZARDS IN GAMES

The job of the wizard in any game, whether tabletop roleplaying or video, is to deal damage—a lot of damage. A wizard without a spell that sends a massive ball of fire at his opponent's face is not much of an asset. The trade-off is that wizards are often "glass cannons," able to deal significant damage, but not able to absorb much of it. It's no accident that the most common type of armor you see on a game wizard is a cloth robe. That said, there are plenty of games that diverge from this paradigm. The wizard in the video game Diablo III, for example, sports articulated metal plating as part of her armor and the traditional robe has been re-imagined as something closer to a long-sleeved tunic with open cuffs and trailing tails. She still has the lowest armor rating of all the classes, suggesting excessive armor would hinder the wizard in channeling arcane power to slaughter her enemies.

The term "wizard" in the Diablo world describes a specific type of spellcaster rather than just a magic user. Blizzard, the maker of Diablo, describes wizards as "renegade spellcasters who use their bodies as vessels for arcane energy, forsaking the more careful path favored by other magic users. They manipulate all manner of forces to disintegrate, burn, and freeze their foes, and they can control time and light to teleport, create powerful illusions, and deflect oncoming attacks."

Collectible Card Games

One other kind of game that exploded in popularity in the 1990s and continues to fascinate millions today is the collectible card game (CCG). Invented by Richard Garfield, a mathematics professor in Washington State, CCGs depend on players each assembling unique decks from cards they've collected. Each type of card has different strengths and weaknesses, and played in combination, they defeat your opponent.

The first and still largest CCG is Magic: The Gathering, with more than 6 million players worldwide. Based in a fantasy world, it offers a scenario in which the two opposing players are dueling wizards, each casting spells and summoning creatures and artifacts to attack the other. The first wizard to drain his or her opponent of life points wins the game.

Parsing out the wizard as a category of spellcaster is a common contrivance of video and tabletop games. Indeed, one of the greatest contributions to wizard lore such interactive and visual media have given us is a vast number of wizarding niches and specializations: abjurer, conjurer, illusionist, psionist, cabalist, battle mage, archmage—any variant of the —mancer suffix: geomancer, pyromancer, telemancer, chronomancer, etc.—the list goes on.

Ḥeal Thy Ally

Classes that can heal the wounds of their allies are usually magic users: bards, clerics, druids, and shamans. Note how healing classes use the same magic resource as the damage-dealers. Wizards can sometimes heal but as a rule prefer to leave that to others.

The variety of wizard is limited only by the imagination of the programmer or the dungeon master. The continuing development of video game technology suggests that wizards in games are going to be with us for a long time to come.

WIZARDS IN COMICS

Kin to the world of gaming media, comic books have given birth to limitless flavors of wizards. Such visual storytelling fired the imaginations of children long before color television and home entertainment. Comics served as a potent visual inspiration for the members of the baby boom generation who pioneered early roleplaying and computer games.

Many of the older generation will recall fondly the age of comics; just as most children today have a gaming console, many children in the mid-twentieth century had a comic book collection. For those of a certain age, comic books filled a similar role that gaming does today, delivering bite-sized visually rich action-adventure and fantasy stories. The popularity of comics was so pervasive it was feared that reading comics was actually contributing to juvenile delinquency, a refrain that seems to shift with the youth trend *du jour*. The doomsayers might have you believe that the industry has been slowing dying since the 1950s, but that ignores the fact that comic book sales are stronger than they've been in years. Certainly, competing media and shifting distribution channels took their toll on comic book sales, but it is still a multimillion-dollar industry and—when factoring in the debut of digital sales—grew almost 90 percent between 2003 and 2013.

It is difficult to find a publication with a longer pedigree. Take the example of Superman, the template for comic book heroes, who made his debut in 1938 and is still featured in various series to this day. Comic books are snapshots of the time in which they were created: the art style, the dialogue, the story arcs, the moods of the characters are all informed by the prevailing culture. You can see this reflection in simple things such as superhero attire that has evolved from primary-colored tights and capes to grungy street clothes and articulated armor. The wizards in comics come in myriad forms as a result of this cultural echo, and we can easily argue they advance more complex notions of wizards and wizardry than their literary counterparts.

Shazam!

Wizards in all their forms are tailor-made for comic books. It's telling that a magazine devoted to comic books and their place in pop culture took the name of *Wizard*. Not only can the artist indulge in rendering bright, flashy spells, but the powers of the wizard clearly align with the powers of the superhero. Flight, teleportation, foresight, augmented strength, elemental control, mind control, transformation—all these types of powers are exhibited in comic book heroes and the wizards discussed in this book.

Of course, there are instances of prototypical wizards in comics complete with flowing beards and mystical powers. Originally drawn for Whiz Comics in 1940, Shazam is a 3,000-year-old wizard who transforms young Billy Batson into Captain Marvel when Billy calls out his name, "Shazam!"

> "No, I would not want to live in a world without dragons, as I would not want to live in a world without magic, for that is a world without mystery, and that is a world without faith."
>
> —DRIZZT DO'URDEN, *STREAMS OF SILVER* BY R.A. SALVATORE

Shazam was conceived as an ancient Egyptian mystic living at the Rock of Eternity, a nexus point of the universe. Sensing that his time on earth was nearly over, he gave the divine powers represented by his name to Billy: S for the wisdom of Solomon; H for the strength of Hercules; A for the stamina of Atlas; Z for the power of Zeus; A for the courage of Achilles; M for the speed of Mercury. When the series was resurrected in the 1970s, due to copyright issues, DC Comics began billing Captain Marvel's adventures under the name Shazam! Ironically, the superhero is so often mistakenly referred to by his mentor's name that DC officially changed Captain Marvel's name to Shazam in 2012.

Dr. Strange

Here's another character who takes his inspiration from wizarding archetypes. Introduced in the early 1960s by Marvel Comics, Doctor Stephen Vincent Strange has the look of heroes of that era with his bright-colored tunic, tights, and trademark high-collar red cape that enables him to fly. A former neurosurgeon, Dr. Strange is an incanter who draws his powers from mystical entities, which allow him to cast certain spells or use mystical objects with exotic sounding names such as Crimson Bands of Cyttorak, the Winds of Watoomb, or the Eye of Agamotto. He serves as the Sorcerer Supreme, the primary protector of earth against magical and mystical threats. Dr. Strange has been described as "the mightiest magician in the cosmos," and he fits the mold of the wizard more closely than many of his peers.

A Wizard by Any Other Name

Many in the comic world eschew the established model of the wizard. Jenny Sparks is a relatively modern take on this, having been created in the 1990s. Sparks is an electromancer: She can draw electricity from devices or even from the human brain, and can also convert her body into pure electricity. Sparks is known as one of DC Comics's Century Babies: supernatural beings birthed at the stroke of midnight on January 1, 1900, who lived through the entire twentieth century. She stopped aging at nineteen, and her moods are tied to the flow of time and the status of the world. Jenny Sparks is portrayed as tough and sassy, often drawn lighting up a cigarette with the electricity cupped in her hands. She was a member of several branches of the British military, leading various superhero teams. She forsakes the classic look of a wizard, preferring late twentieth-century urban clothing with her signature Union Jack T-shirt, but as a manipulator of the elements, her wizarding roots are evident.

X-Men Wizards

The X-Men are one of the most enduring comic franchises, spawning multiple story arcs and several live-action films. So many heroes from the X-Men universe could fall under the wizard rubric that it would be impractical to list them all in this book. A few of the more notable wizard-like X-Men include:

- Storm, manipulator of weather
- Jean Grey, a telepathic telekinetist
- Magneto, master of electromagnetism
- Firestar the pyromancer
- Kitty Pryde, who has the rare skill of self-transmutation
- Professor X, the series namesake, a high-level telepath who can read, control, and influence minds

Wizard Villains

Unsurprisingly, wizards also make great comic book villains. Dr. Victor von Doom is nominally the archvillain of the Fantastic Four, but he has transcended his original franchise and is featured in other Marvel products including films, video games, and television series; he was ranked as the Fourth Greatest Villain on *Wizard* magazine's "100 Greatest Villains of All Time" list. A scientist by trade, Dr. Doom has managed over time to learn a considerable amount of mystical and magical skills. He is capable of energy projection, psionic transfer of his consciousness, and technopathic control over certain machines, and is possessed of exceptionally strong willpower. In addition, Dr. Doom uses his scientific genius to steal or replicate the abilities of other beings—famously appropriating the powers of the Silver Surfer—and he  wears armor that augments his physical strength to superhuman levels.

Doom is rather far from the stereotype of the wizard, and he seems to conform only in the sense that he is generally a user of magic—and even then his power is largely cerebral versus corporeal. That said, it is fairly easy to see the wizardry he practices as an augmented form of science, evoking the alchemical tradition that blurred the lines between truth and fantasy.

And then there are those characters who fall somewhere in between. John Constantine is known for his cynicism, deadpan snark, ruthless cunning, constant chain-smoking, and being one of the greatest wizards in comics history. Antihero of the Hellblazer series, Constantine plays the part of occult detective in the great game between heaven and hell. De facto on the side of good, he is just as likely to con an angel as a demon, although the point is frequently made that he is driven by a desire to do good.

Unlike other comic book wizards, Constantine rarely uses magical spells, preferring to best his enemies with his quick wits. That is not to say, however, that he is not familiar with many schools of magic: He employs an array of spells, charms, and occult objects, including the supernatural ability to make his own luck. First penned in the 1980s, Constantine initially has a certain James Bond style, but later iterations take a darker approach culminating in the 2005 film starring geek-favorite Keanu Reeves. As comics are wont to do, John Constantine challenges our concept of a wizard. He muddles the lines between good and evil that are usually clearly drawn in the genre.

WIZARDS BEFORE OUR EYES

Visually based media, where magic can be rendered with color and fury, is the perfect showcase for wizards. Comic book heroes, avatars of roleplaying games . . . these are forms in which wizards shine. Given the incredible growth of the gaming industry, it's a sure bet that new games, many featuring their own versions of the wizard—such as Carbine's WildStar, with psionic Espers and pistol-wielding Spellslingers—will continue to come online. The proliferation of wizarding types in modern games stems from deep roots in our collective culture, and we need only look back through the pages of this book to understand why the wizarding archetype is so commonplace in games.

Wizards All Around Us

"That's the thing about magic; you've got to know it's still here, all around us, or it just stays invisible for you."

—CHARLES DE LINT, *DREAMS UNDERFOOT*

hroughout this book we have considered primarily wizards of lore and legend. However, there have been real-life wizards as well. We've mentioned a few of them: John Dee, Cagliostro, Nicholas Flamel, Paracelsus, and others. Before we end, we should consider one more, a man who had a profound impact on modern wizardry: Aleister Crowley.

ALEISTER CROWLEY

Crowley became notorious in the twentieth century as an exponent of magic and mysticism, and all sorts of absurd rumors swirled around him: He regularly performed black masses, he was in league with the devil, and so on.

In truth, Crowley, born in England in 1875 to a highly religious family, became fascinated in his youth with mystical spiritual experiences. In 1898, he joined the Hermetic Order of the Golden Dawn, an organization founded ten years previously on the teachings of Hermes Trismegistus, though it also incorporated elements of the Kabbalah, alchemy, astrology, and other elements of Eastern mystical traditions. He became a protégé of the Golden Dawn leader Allan Bennett, who introduced him to drug use as a way of heightening his consciousness and making him more open to spiritual experiences.

The Book of the Law

In 1904, while Crowley and his wife, Rose, were in Egypt, Rose became possessed by a messenger of the god Horus named Aiwass. The spirit dictated a book to Crowley, which was titled *The Book of the Law,* and this work became the keystone of Crowley's later philosophy. Crowley announced himself the prophet of a new age for humanity, the Aeon of Horus. Magic was central to this, and Crowley defined it as "the art and science of causing change to occur in conformity with Will." Later he founded a community in Sicily, which he called The Abbey of Thelema ("thelema" is the Greek word for "will").

As he developed his ideas further, he published a series of books, including *Magick in Theory and Practice and Magick Without Tears.* Much of his magical practice was devoted to sex magick, which he believed was essential to gain higher knowledge.

He traveled extensively, including to China, to northern Africa, to Europe, and to the United States. He was often accused of being a Satanist, and he encouraged these sorts of rumors, though he was not. He suffered from poverty and, increasingly, from addiction to heroin and died in 1947.

Crowley's influence on modern mysticism has been considerable. Various organizations of his disciples continue to be active to this day, and his works have remained in print and are widely read. So we can see, even in our world of computers, smartphones, and space stations there is a place for wizards and their magic.

A WIZARD'S JOURNEY

The story of wizards takes us from the beginning of our species to the latest video game technology. It's a journey spanning thousands of years and countless traditions, civilizations, nations, languages, and artifacts. That's because being a wizard is at the heart of what we want to be. We want to control our own destinies with magic, to summon strength from the earth, nourishment from the heavens, and fire from the stars. Throughout human history, we've longed for such power. But, like the power put in our hands through the advances of science, we recognize that it can be dangerous.

Scientific wizardry split the atom and began to open to us the secrets of the universe. It also leveled the cities of Hiroshima and Nagasaki and presented us, for the first time in humankind's history, with the power to destroy our species. Perhaps for this reason, we see wizards often standing between the light and the dark. They can be awesome allies— as in the case of Gandalf, Dumbledore, or Harry Potter. They can be equally terrifying foes: Voldemort, Saruman, Dr. Doom.

Precisely because they represent this duality in our own nature, wizards will always be with us. They will inhabit human lore and legends as long as there are people to tell tales and remember stories. And we can be sure that every time we start down a dark corridor, not knowing what's at the other end, whenever we're faced with a door and hear a soft, ominous creaking on the other side, or whenever we're faced with the unknown . . . someone will turn to the wizard and say, "You go first!"

Index

A

Abjuration, 195
The Aeneid, 84, 102–4
Akamatsu, Ken, 115
Alchemists, 11, 40–44,
  87, 131
Apollonius of Tyana,
  88–89
Arneson, Dave, 192–93
Arthurian legends, 43,
  55, 67–79, 175, 180–81.
  See also Merlin
Arthurian poem, 71–72
Astrology, 31–33
Athames, 55–56
Atlantes, 39

B

Baba Yaga, 111–12
Bacon, Roger, 42
Bakshi, Ralph, 175–76,
  182
Ballantine fantasy novels,
  150
Bartimaeus series, 23,
  28, 149
Baum, Frank L., 59
Belgariad series, 13, 20,
  26, 56, 159–61
Bennett, Allan, 217

Bewitched, 187
Bloch, Robert, 47
Book of the Law, 217–18
Books, wizards in,
  118–71
Boorman, John, 26, 27,
  49, 72, 180–81
Bradley, Marion Zimmer,
  66, 79
Bramah, Ernest, 150
Brooks, Terry, 149
Buffy the Vampire Slayer,
  80, 188–89
Butcher, Jim, 21, 148,
  162–64

C

Cagliostro, Conte di, 42,
  104–5, 216
The Canterbury Tales,
  93–94
Card games, 28–29, 207
*The Case of Charles Dexter
  Ward*, 29, 62, 166–68
Casting lots, 84
Cauldrons, 53, 56
Caves, 48–49
Cellini, Benvenuto, 61
Chalice, 56
Charmed, 60, 189–90
Chaucer, Geoffrey, 93–94

Chronicles of Narnia
  series, 153–54, 158
Circe, 15–16, 51
Clarke, Susanna, 149,
  205
Clavicula Salomonis,
  95–96
Clothing/robes, 56–58
Comic book wizards,
  114–16, 191–93, 201,
  208–14
Conan the Barbarian,
  177–79
Conjuration, 147, 195
*A Connecticut Yankee in
  King Arthur's Court*,
  73, 79
Crimson King, 40
Crowley, Aleister, 50, 58,
  216–18
Crystal balls, 58–59, 97,
  174
The Crystal Cave, 13, 49,
  79, 149
Crystals, 59
Curse tablets, 84–85

D

"Dark Eidolon," 165–66
Dark Tower series, 40
Darwath Trilogy, 13

De Boron, Robert, 69
Dee, John, 42, 58–59, 97–98, 216
Deryni series, 149
Diablo series, 200–201, 206–7
Discworld series, 22, 149
Divination, 25, 30–33, 112, 179, 195
Dr. Doom, 212–14
Dr. Faustus, 98–100
Dr. Strange, 211
Dolls, magical, 84–85
Dragonlance series, 14, 56–57, 101, 149, 169–71
Dreams, 33, 113–14
Dresden Files series, 21, 48, 58, 94, 148, 162–64
Dung beetle magic, 98
Dungeons & Dragons (cartoon), 187–88
Dungeons & Dragons (film), 14, 185–86
Dungeons & Dragons (game), 6, 25, 169–70, 192–98
Dunsany, Lord, 150
Dwelling places, 48–49

E

Earthsea stories, 149, 155–57, 166
Eddings, David, 12–13, 20, 26, 56, 155, 159–61
Elder Scrolls, 201
Emerald Tablet, 43
Enlightenment, 104–5

Equipment for wizards
athames, 55–56
cauldrons, 53, 56
chalice, 56
clothing, 56–58
crystal balls, 59
herbs/roots, 61–62
magic circles, 60–61
pentacles, 54–55
pentagrams, 54–56
robes, 56–58
runes, 58–59
spellbooks, 60, 62–63
staff, 51–53
swords, 55–56
wands, 51–53, 56
Everquest, 203
Evocations, 25, 28–30, 62, 96, 195
Excalibur, 15, 26, 27, 49, 72, 75–76, 79, 180–81
Exorcists, 112–13

F

Familiars, 46–47
Fantasia, 38, 175
Fantasy, beginnings of, 149–52
Faust, 69, 98–101
Faustian pact, 101
Films, wizards in, 75–80, 172–90
Final Fantasy series, 204–5
Flamel, Nicholas, 6, 42, 216
Fowles, John, 36

G

Gambon, Michael, 184
Garfield, Richard, 207
Gauntlet, 200
Geoffrey of Monmouth, 67–68
Goethe, Johann Wolfgang von, 38, 100
Grossman, Lev, 22, 82, 157–59
Gygax, Gary, 192–93, 197

H

Hambly, Barbara, 13
Harris, Richard, 184
Harry Dresden series, 21, 48, 58, 94, 148, 162–64
Harry Potter series, 7, 10, 25–26, 30–32, 41, 46, 51, 56, 94, 118–47
Healers, 43, 113, 204, 208
Herbs, 61–62
Hermes, 85–86, 217
Hermeticism, 86–88, 217
Hickman, Tracy, 14–15, 149, 169–71
The History of the Kings of Britain, 67–68
The Hobbit (book), 19, 149–53
The Hobbit (film), 181–83
The Hollow Hills, 81, 149
Howard, Robert E., 177–79

I

The Idylls of the King, 71
Illusion, 34, 36, 56, 195
Incantations, 25–27, 62,
    84, 97, 103, 122, 125,
    132
Incense, 97
Isengard, 48, 52

J

Jackson, Peter, 7, 173,
    176, 181, 183–85
Jenny Sparks comics,
    211–12
Joan of Arc, 91
*Jonathan Strange and Mr
    Norrell*, 149, 205

K

Key of Solomon, 95–96
King, Stephen, 40
King Arthur, 78
Koschei the Deathless,
    109–11
Kurtz, Katherine, 149

L

The Last Enchantment,
    72, 149
Le Carre, John, 73
Legend of Zelda series,
    202–3

Le Guin, Ursula K., 143,
    149, 155–57, 166
Lemegeton, 95–97
Le Morte d'Arthur, 70, 79
Lévi, Eliphas, 105–6
Lewis, C.S., 13, 52, 101,
    149, 153–54, 158
*The Lion, the Witch, and
    the Wardrobe*, 52, 153
The Lord of the Rings
    (book), 13–14, 19–20,
    36–37, 149–50, 152
The Lord of the Rings
    (film series), 7, 176, 181,
    183–85
Lovecraft, H.P., 29, 62,
    166–68
Lucas, George, 157, 173

M

Macbeth, 53
Magic
    power of, 24–49
    types of, 25–27
    world of, 9–23
Magical dolls, 84–85
Magic circles, 28, 60–61,
    95–96
The Magician's Nephew,
    101, 149, 153, 154
The Magicians series,
    157–59
The Magic Sword, 174–75
Magic: The Gathering,
    28–29, 207
Magus, 35–37
The Magus, 36

Magus, Simon, 90–91
Majere, Caramon, 15
Majere, Raistlin, 14–15,
    23, 101, 149, 169–71,
    197
Mallorean series, 13,
    159–61
Malory, Thomas, 70, 79
Manga wizards, 114–16
Marlowe, Christopher,
    98–100
Masters of the Universe,
    179
McKellen, Ian, 183–84
McKillip, Patricia, 149
Merlin
    Arthurian legends,
        43, 55, 67–79, 175,
        180–81
    in films/movies, 75–80
    on television, 75,
        79–81
Merlin (book), 69
Merlin (film), 79–80
"Merlin and Vivien,"
    71–72
Merlin's Apprentice, 79–80
Middle Ages, 88–94
Milius, John, 177–78
Mr. Merlin, 187
The Mists of Avalon, 66, 79
MMORPG games, 203–6.
    See also Video games
Monkey King, 108–9
*Monty Python and the Holy
    Grail*, 76
Morris, William, 149, 150

Movies, wizards in, 75–
80, 172–90

N

Narnia books, 153–54,
158
Necromancy, 29–30, 57,
98, 195, 199, 203
Neill, Sam, 79–80
Novels, wizards in,
148–71

O

Orlando Furioso, 39

P

Paracelsus, 42, 58, 167,
216
Pentacles, 54–55
Pentagrams, 54–56
Philosopher's Stone, 42,
43
Pratchett, Terry, 22, 24,
57, 149, 172
Prospero, 17–18, 59

R

Rainmakers, 113
Relics, 92–95
Renaissance, 95–98
Robes, 56–58
Roots/herbs, 61–62
Rowling, J.K., 6–7, 21, 27,
118–47, 157–58

Runes, 58–59
RuneScape, 203

S

Shakespeare, William,
17–18, 53, 59
Shamans, 45–47, 112–13,
208
Shannara series, 149
Shapeshifters, 37–38,
131–32, 164, 202
Shazam, 209–11
Simon the Magician,
90–91
Smith, Clark Ashton,
165–66
Sorcerers, 37–40
"Sorcerer's Apprentice,"
38, 40, 175
Sorcery, 23, 38, 101,
169–70, 177
Spellbooks, 60, 62–63
Spellcasting, 62–63, 196
Spirits, summoning,
28–30, 96
Staff, 51–53
Star Trek, 47, 193
Star Wars, 157, 173
Stewart, Mary, 13, 23, 43,
49, 58, 72, 79, 81, 149
Straub, Peter, 40
Stroud, Jonathan, 23, 28,
149
Summoning spirits,
28–30, 96
The Sword in the Stone, 13,
22, 77, 175

Swords, 55–56. *See also*
Excalibur
Symbols, 34, 48, 52, 54,
58–59

T

Tablets, curse, 84–85
Tabula Smaragdina, 43
Tarot deck, 34–35
Television wizards, 60,
75–76, 79–81, 172, 182,
187–90
The Tempest, 17–18
Tennyson, Lord Alfred,
71
*Tinker, Tailor, Soldier,
Spy*, 73
Tolkien, J.R.R., 10, 19,
30, 48, 52, 57, 59, 70,
149–53
Transmutation, 56, 195
Trismegistus, Hermes,
85–88, 217
Twain, Mark, 73–75

U

Ultima Online, 203

V

Video games, 191–208,
214
Virgil, 102–4
*The Voyage of the Dawn
Treader*, 13, 149, 153

W

Wands, 10, 51–53, 56, 62, 94
Warlocks, 136–37, 189, 199–201, 206
Weis, Margaret, 14–15, 149, 169–71
White, T.H., 13, 22, 47, 77, 175, 183
Witchcraft, 18, 55, 73, 91, 136–37, 140, 189
Wizard Magazine, 212
A Wizard of Earthsea, 149, 155–57, 166
Wizardry
  dark side of, 14–18
  hazards of, 23
  in Middle Ages, 88–94
  modern wizardry, 94
  nineteenth-century wizardry, 105–6
  in Renaissance era, 95–98
Wizards
  animal helpers for, 46–47
  in books, 118–71
  in China, 112–14
  classes for, 21–23, 51, 123, 136, 138–40
  in comic books, 114–16, 191–93, 201, 208–14
  dwelling places of, 48–49
  of East, 107–16
  equipment for, 50–63
  examples of, 10–23
  explanation of, 10–12
  in films/movies, 75–80, 172–90
  gods and, 20–21
  of history, 65–81
  in Japan, 114–16
  journey of, 218–19
  levels of, 11
  life of, 12–13
  manga wizards, 114–16
  in Middle Ages, 88–94
  in nineteenth century, 105–6
  in novels, 148–71
  in popular culture, 6–7
  relics of, 94–95
  in Renaissance, 95–98
  robes for, 56–58
  in Russia, 109–12
  on television, 60, 75–76, 79–81, 172, 182, 187–90
  types of, 10–11
  in video games, 191–208, 214
  of West, 82–106
Wizards (film), 175–76
Wizards and Warriors, 187
The Wizards of Waverly Place, 190
The Wonderful Wizard of Oz, 59, 137
World of Warcraft (WoW), 205–6

X

X-Men comics, 212

Z

Zodiac signs, 33